SHE'S ALL I NEED

CHIQUITA DENNIE

304 PUBLISHING COMPANY

This book is dedicated to my family, especially (Rhonda Dennie, Grandma, and Aunt Marcia) for always believing in me. Also, I want to shout out my big Brent Dennie, JD, Christopher, Lil James, Jazzypoo, my sisters, and best friends from Memphis: Nita, San, Reese, Jennifer, LA besties Tavi & Tiffany for always supporting me. Shout out to all of my cousins, nieces, and nephews.

"Starting small can lead to bigger things."

—Chiquita Dennie

LATEST RELEASES FROM CHIQUITA DENNIE

Latest Releases from Chiquita Dennie
    Antonio and Sabrina: Struck in Love 1, 2, 3,4
    Heart of Stone, Book 1 (Emery & Jackson)
    Heart of Stone Book 1.5 Emery &Jackson A Valentine's
Day Short
    Janice and Carlo: Captivated By His Love
    Heart of Stone, Book 2 (Jordan and Damon)
    Temptation
    Heart of Stone, Book 3 (Angela and Brent)
    Bossy Billionaire
    Cocky Catcher
    Joaquin Fuertes (Fuertes Cartel Book 1)
    ReFuel
    Pressure
    Upcoming Releases (2021/2022):
    Heart of Stone, Book 4 Jessica and Joseph
    Joaquin Fuertes (Fuertes Cartel Book 2)
    She's All I Need
    Exposed - A Salvation Society Novel

Dare To Love
Mutual Agreement
Something Gained

DISCLAIMER

This work of fiction contains strong language and explicit sexual content and is only intended for mature readers. This story may contain unconventional situations, language, and sexual encounters that may offend some readers.This book is for mature readers (18+).

Are you signed up for my newsletter?

Join today and find out all the latest in new releases, contests, giveaways, sneak peeks and more.

https://landing.mailerlite.com/webforms/landing/r7j2s6

SYNOPSIS

Donovan is an all-star football player—the kind of man every woman wants—but he only has eyes for Kamara. The trouble is the media scrutiny—and other's opinions—have already set them up for failure.

Kamara is intelligent, quirky, an accomplished journalist in her own right, and not the kind of woman most athletes would consider girlfriend material, but when she falls for her best friend's brother, a handsome football player, all the so-called rules go out the window.

When they break up, their lives become even more complicated. Donovan fights to win her back, but only if he can win her trust back and get her away from the new prying eyes of an old enemy.

Will Donovan and Kamara get their second-chance romance? Or have things already gone too far?

The sweat beads poured down my face as I watched the clock run down on the scoreboard. I mentally calculated if the play I was about to execute would get us to the win we'd been working for the entire season.

"Bro you ready? All eyes on you," Savion Jennings, my best friend and the running back for our team, asked me. We've played together for the last four years on the Los Angeles Hawks professional football league. I splashed the water on my face and slid my helmet back on and listened as the coach ran down the play.

"Donovan stay focused and you got this," Coach Bryce remarked, clapping me on the shoulder.

"1, 2, 3, Hawks!" all of us yelled. We ran out on the field and lined up.

I looked up to the bleachers and saw my good-luck charm sitting there, talking animatedly with her hands. She rolled her eyes, and I grinned, knowing that just her presence was what I needed to get this last play and win the game.

Kamara was best friends with my sister, Luna. They met in college, and they now worked together writing for the local newspaper, the *Los Angeles Life*. Luna, my feisty little sister, had loved fashion growing up, and now her dream job kept her in that field as a columnist who got to go to fashion shows and talk about clothes every day.

Kamara Powell was a quirky, intelligent, magna cum laude graduate from Columbia, with a degree in journalism. She was all about exposing real world problems, finding corruption, and exposing politicians or business corporations that screwed over the little guy.

"Hut one, hut two, hike! Hike!" I called in the huddle and jogged backwards, holding the ball in a tight grip. I looked from side to side and caught Savion at the 30-yard line, holding his hands up. I tossed the ball and watched as it flew out of my sweaty hands. I glanced at the clock. There were forty seconds left. The Atlanta Scorpions were running toward Savion. I scanned the crowd again and saw Kamara, standing with the other fans, watching as the ball seemed to move in slow motion toward his hands. Savion jumped off the ground and finally made contact, then turned around and took off down to the 20-yard line, then the 10, as the clock counted down from forty seconds.

The Atlanta Scorpions made impact, but Savion held onto the ball and made it to the end zone for a touchdown as the clock ran out. I pumped my fist in the air in appreciation of having the best team on the planet to play with as their quarterback.

"That's what I'm talking about!" Reuben Atkinson, our other friend, ran over and gave me a bear hug.

"Shit," I muttered, releasing a long-held breath once the ball made it to its destination.

The reporters ran toward us and started hounding us

with questions, as we met Savion and slapped hands in celebration as a team.

"Donovan! Congrats on winning the Nationals. What do you think of your Super Bowl chances?" asked Ben Simmons, the jerk reporter of FSNG Sports. He pushed his microphone in my face.

I glared, not up to answering questions. Every other night, he broadcasted about our team, or how I'm paid all these millions of dollars and barely got a big game ring.

I'd been playing football all my life since I was kid, then through high school and college. My parents saw something in me and nurtured my passion. They put me into every after-school program they could think of, and it only motivated me to get into the big leagues. My parents, Patricia and Llyod Hunt, still came to my games when they weren't working at the hardware store they'd owned since I was ten.

Now, at thirty-two, I was a Super Bowl Champion, but the media didn't respect me until I was in the league for over seven years and won two championship trophies and MVP. I could admit that I did tend to go at the reporters sometimes on social media or in the locker rooms, when I felt disrespected, but it was only when I was pushed, and I had to push back.

"No comment," I said, waving him off. He thought I wouldn't remember him talking about me possibly taking performance enhancement drugs to get our ring two years ago. When it hit the media circuit I wanted to go up to the station and kick his ass, but the coach, players, and my parents talked me out of doing it because it would just lead to more drama in the papers.

"Everyone had the game going into overtime Donovan, what do you think about your big game chances?"

The lights of the camera glared in my face as more

photographers and news outlets surrounded us near the corner of the field toward the locker rooms.

"I think you'll have to wait and see like everyone else," I replied, starting to walk off toward my parents sitting in the bleachers with Luna and Kamara.

"Come on Donovan, they pay you the big bucks. The least you could do is answer a question," Ben chastised and shoved the mic in my face again and I slapped it away.

"Get that microphone out of my face. I told you, no comment."

He grinned. "Funny, you get paid the most money, and you got the least personality," Ben joked. The other reporters chuckled.

"Fuck you," I muttered under my breath.

"What was that? Did pretty boy get upset?" Ben taunted and tried to antagonize me.

"That's enough, Ben. You're doing too much for a guy who hates this team," Savion said, clapping me on the shoulder to steer me away from a fight. He knew how I was when it came to the bullshit celebrity lifestyle; I didn't give a damn about anything but my family and teammates. Everything else was irrelevant to me. For one thing, I'd never kissed anybody's ass to get ahead, and I wouldn't start with him.

"Tell your boy to watch that arm!" Ben called out as he walked away from us. I made a mental note to have my agent find out what Ben's gripe with me was about because over the years, it had only gotten worse between us. He had been reporting on our team for over six years—and specifically, talking trash about my abilities as a quarterback.

"Hit the showers, boys." Coach Harrison motioned for us to head back to the locker room.

Everyone screamed, shouted, and congratulated each other as security escorted us through the locker room hallway. They pushed the door open, and I went straight to my locker and removed my helmet and pads, then headed to the shower. Savion did his usual thing, rocking out to music after a win to get the entire locker room pumped up. I saw the champagne bottles coming out as I turned the corner to the showers. I turned the water on steaming hot and stood underneath to let it run down my back and along my sore muscles and aches. I saw purple bruises on my thighs and stomach from the back-to-back hits. I grabbed the soap, washed up, and prayed I had some leftovers at the house, or I'd probably have to order in because I wasn't coming back out. I knew Savion wanted to go out and celebrate, but I wasn't in the mood anymore. Something about that cocky smirk on Ben's face told me he was up to something.

"Yo, Donovan, your sister's looking for you," explained Jimmy, the offensive lineman.

I nodded, finished cleaning up, and turned the water off. I placed a towel around my waist, dried my hair, and stepped out, then went back into the locker room. It was chaos—full of reporters, loud music, and everybody talking over each other. I shook my head and changed clothes fast, keeping my head down as much as possible.

"D! Hold up." Savion jumped down off the bench and pushed through the crowd.

"What's up?" I pushed through the double doors, looking for my sister.

"You coming out with us to the bar?" Savion asked.

"Nope."

I saw Luna standing with her friends that I got tickets for. She saw me and ran into my arms almost knocking me down.

"Congratulations! You did it again, Donovan!" Luna screamed, hugging me around my neck.

Luna was twenty-eight, and she'd always had terrible taste in men. Either she would find out they cheated on her, or they would dump her because she wasn't connected with me and the lifestyle that came with the job. Luna was a spitfire; she was 5'4", with long auburn hair, and the biggest dewy eyes that could break my heart and bank account in a split-second. I spoiled her rotten, and I didn't regret it one bit; Luna had worked hard through school and while starting her career as a writer.

Next to her was the most beautiful woman I had ever met. Kamara Powell was the type of woman who made me want to give her my all and protect her. She stood at 5'8" with shoulder-length blond hair, chestnut brown skin, full lips with a pronounced Cupid's bow, deep-set black eyes that could have me confessing my entire life story whenever she stared at me, a cute button nose, a square-shaped face, and dimples in her cheeks. It was funny to me how I would always start a stupid argument with her just to hear her silky, sexy voice.

We were complete opposites in every way because she was all about saving the world in some capacity and would talk to anyone she met—no matter where she was. Her personality was outgoing and sweet.

Me, on the other hand, I didn't like people beyond my family and close friends. I had been burned too many times by people, and I had closed off my trust—until she came into my life.

"Thanks, Luna. Where's Mom and Dad?" I asked, keeping my eyes on Kamara, who was talking to another guy. I knew he went to college with them, but I didn't know how close they were or if it was something more.

.   .   .

"THEY COULDN'T MAKE it because Dad had to work at the shop to cover for Brandon's wife having the baby," Luna informed. I pulled my keys out of my pocket and started to head to my car, when a group of girls approached us.

"Donovan can we please have your autograph?" one of the girls asked, holding a photo of me.

"Sure."

"Me, too, but right here." She lifted her shirt up and showed off her breasts covered in her black bra. My eyes widened in shock, and I heard a gasp come from beside us. I turned, and it was Kamara, rolling her eyes. She started to leave without Luna.

"Damn. You want my autograph, too?" Savion mumbled. I chuckled.

"I'd love to have you both," the redhead blurted out.

We looked at each other, knowing what she really meant. I was known in the media as somewhat of a play-boy, but I'd never cheated on a girl or shared women with my friends. Surprisingly, I was a one-woman type of guy when I found someone I liked. Did I have casual sex often? Yes, but I was still young and not settling down any time soon.

"Not happening sweetie, put your boobs away and have some type of respect for his family standing next to him," Luna complained.

"That's enough Luna, let's go." I stretched my arm around her shoulder and pulled her into me and stepped out of the halls with security walking in front to keep more fans at bay.

"What are you about to do now?" Luna questioned as we left the stadium.

"I need to crash and eat. How did you get up here?" I wondered, looked behind me as Kamara came out of the door behind us with the same guy. I groaned annoyed she was still paying him any type of attention. I wanted her focused on me only and nobody else. I know it was stupid when she wasn't even my girl and hated my guts, but I didn't care.

"Kamara's sister dropped us off before she went to work," Luna informed me.

My Dad had made me promise not to get Luna another car because she'd crashed the last one. So, she had to catch rides with friends or family—unless Kamara drove her car, but Luna had told me it was in the shop right now. Her older sister, Porsha, was a nurse and worked afternoon and night shifts, so it was easy for her to get them up there on her way to the hospital.

"All right, get in the car."

"Hit me up tomorrow, bro," Savion said, slapping my hand before jogging to his bike.

"Kamara you ready!" Luna called out.

"I'm riding with Doug, Luna," Kamara said and I groaned, not ready to get into a fight with her.

"Get in the car, Kamara," I rushed out, holding the passenger door open.

"I can get myself home," Kamara responded, hands on her hips.

I walked over to her, peered into her piercing eyes, and almost lost my breath.

"You came here with my sister; I don't know this guy from the doorman at my building," I lied. I knew Thomas, the doorman at my condo, and his wife and three kids, but she didn't know that.

"I'm a grown woman who can take care of herself," Kamara snapped back.

I wanted to reply that I could see she was a grown woman, with her full curves covered in her oversized sweater, and her tights that she wore with her boots, and her long hair, layered over her large breasts. I bit my lip, trying to control my thoughts from coming out of my mouth. "Kamara, why do you have to fight me on everything? Just get in the car."

"Kamara please get in the car before he acts like an ass out here," Luna pleaded, knowing how I got if I didn't get my way. I wouldn't call myself an asshole, but I do have my ways to get what I want.

"Fine. Only because it's you, Luna. Doug, I'll call you later," Kamara said, waving bye to him.

"Not if I can help it," I muttered to myself.

"What did you say?" Kamara asked.

"Nothing," I replied, holding the door open for her and my sister.

I went to the driver's side of my Jeep and jumped in. I glanced through the rearview mirror at Kamara, biting on her fingernails nervously. I thought it was cute. I turned the radio up and backed out of the parking space, then drove out of the stadium before it could get too crowded with people leaving. I headed to the red light that led out to the street traffic.

Luna turned around in her seat.

"Are you coming to my place or going home?" she asked Kamara.

"Home," Kamara said.

We made eye contact in the mirror and she rolled her eyes and I chuckled. Luna hit me in the chest.

"What's so funny?" Luna had a sneaky look on her face.

"Nothing, put Kamara's address in the navigation center."

She typed in her address, and I hit the freeway from downtown Los Angeles, heading toward Glendale on the 101. Our parents lived in Calabasas and came down for my games often. Luna stayed in North Hollywood. So, family gatherings were few and far between with my schedule.

I took another glance in the mirror, and Kamara's head was leaned back against the seat, staring out the window. I tried to think of something to get her interested in having a conversation with me and decided that I would pick her brain about that Doug character.

"Who's Doug?" I said out loud to no one in particular.

Luna and Kamara looked at me. "A friend from the office," Luna answered.

I nodded, drumming my fingers on the steering wheel to Coldplay's latest song. "Is he your boyfriend?" I asked Luna. Hopefully, she'd answer yes, and my curiosity would be fulfilled for the day.

"Nope. I'm single and not looking for anything," Luna replied.

"What about you, Kamara?" I switched lanes, getting off the freeway ramp.

"I don't date," Kamara replied.

"What? Why?"

"Here we go," Luna groaned, covered her face with her hand and lowered herself in the seat.

"Men unfortunately aren't to my level of being able to handle me," Kamara said, shrugging her shoulders.

"What level?"

"Please don't start her on this conversation Donovan," Luna begged right when I pulled up out front of her apartment building.

"The level that you'll never learn about. Call me when you get home, Luna." Kamara rushed out, opened then closed the door, walked up to her apartment, and stepped inside a few minutes later.

"Just tell her you're in love with her already," Luna commented and I grunted, nudging her in the shoulder.

"I don't love her."

"Donovan you're always pissing her off and then get mad when you see any guy talking to her or in her space."

"I do that with you too. As a big brother I need to make sure you're protected."

Luna waved me off and turned the radio to a different station. I shook my head, got back on the freeway, and headed to her place.

A little while later, I pulled into my garage and turned my Jeep off. I stepped out with my gym bag and headed inside to the elevator. I wasn't ready to purchase a house—even though I had the money to do so—because I wanted to do that with someone once I found the girl who I would spend the rest of my life with. Until then, the expensive Beverly Hills condo would have to be my place of residence. They had all the great amenities, like a pool, gym, media center, and private balconies. I even had the top floor, which held a second level, where my bedroom was, and there was a second bedroom and bathroom downstairs.

I slid my key into the lock and dropped the bag near the door, then fell face-first onto the couch and released a long-held yawn. I was beyond exhausted and would have to take the next few days off to relax and catch up on my sleep before we had to practice for the big game.

I could feel myself drifting off to sleep when my phone buzzed. I lifted it out of my pocket and saw that Luna was texting me.

Luna: Congrats again. Love you!

Me: Thanks, bighead.

Luna: Fuck you.

Me: Telling Mom you cursed.

Luna: Telling Kamara you slept with our friend Kingsley from college.

I wiped my eyes to make sure I read her message correctly. That was a secret I didn't think anyone knew about, but me and Kingsley. We slept together once and that was because she and I ended up at a party together and I didn't know she and my sister were friends at the time.

Me: Don't get your ass kicked, little girl.

Luna: LOL! Love you, too, big bro.

I started to respond but decided to leave it alone for now and close the message thread. I rose from the couch and sauntered to the bedroom to kick off my shoes and drop my pants and shirt in the hamper. I headed into the bathroom for a shower, and then bed.

The doorbell was driving me crazy and pulling me out of the best dream I'd had in a long time. I threw the covers off my head and checked the time on my Apex watch.

"8 AM," I grunted, tossing the covers to the side. I ran a hand over my hair and stretched. I hadn't had a good night's sleep in a long time, and someone had decided to show up at my place early in the morning to ruin what little moments I had to myself before I had to show up at practice. My stomach grumbled, and I adjusted my shaft in my boxers, then picked up my shirt and sweats from the dresser to answer the door. Whoever was knocking was pissing me off. I was glad to not have a lot of neighbors near me on the top floor, with the way they kept ringing the doorbell.

I yanked the door open and glared at Savion, Reuben, and Paolo, our other friend from college. He didn't take the football route like us and pursued a business degree instead. Now, he was my agent.

"Someone looks grumpy." Savion held up a bag of food

and lifted his brows, pushed the door wider and stepped inside.

"Blame Savion. I needed to talk about a business opportunity," Paolo said. He was wearing his usual suit and tie.

"Do you not believe in calling first?"

Savion flopped down on the couch, kicked his legs up and passed the boxes of food around.

I shut the door and went to the back to brush my teeth and wash my face before I kicked him out. I checked my phone and saw missed calls from Paolo, Savion, and Reuben discussing something. I saw notification alerts and clicked on one of the articles with my name as the headline.

"Football star signing boobs like a rock star. Give me a break," Ben Simmons said.

"Can big game come to the Los Angeles Hawks once again?" The news article mentioned. I mumbled to myself.

"After ten years in the league, is he washed up?" I repeated the third headline that was talking about me.

I threw my phone on the bed and headed to the bathroom. I stared in the mirror. I'd turned thirty-two not long ago, and I had plans to possibly retire when I hit thirty-five if I didn't love the game anymore. I was starting to think that might come sooner if I had to deal with that bullshit.

Finally dressed, I went back to the living room and kicked Savion's feet off the table. He flipped me off. I grabbed the extra box of food that was left for me and took a bite of the omelet and pancakes.

Savion was the joker of the group and didn't take things too seriously—unless it involved football. We'd been best friends since high school, and our families had stayed in touch over the years after his parents divorced while he was in college.

Reuben was the baby of the bunch, with his long hair

always up in a bun on top of his head. He had a knack for getting us caught up into trouble. No matter where we went, he'd either be flirting with some girl, making her boyfriend jealous, or possibly having girls fight over him.

Then we had Paolo, the serious one out of all four of us, and we liked to call him "Preacher" since he was always the go-to person for advice and was always preaching about how we should be living our lives without multiple women and sticking to one woman instead.

Me, I was a mixture of all of them, and they called me "Champ" because I was always scoring in some way.

"You see the article?" Paola asked.

I nodded with my mouth full of food. Paolo knew I didn't do interviews or kiss ass. So, he was trying to test the waters to see if I'll respond. I won't, especially knowing Simmons will just keep poking.

"He's trying to piss me off."

"Yeah, but it doesn't help that you buy into his ways," Savion replied, sipping on his orange juice. I grabbed one out of the box on the floor, twisted the top and gulped it down.

"He has it out for you, D. What did you do? Sleep with his girl or something?" Reuben questioned, then stole a piece of bacon off Savion's plate and tossed it in his mouth.

I leaned back in the chair and thought about what I could have done to cause him so much aggravation, but nothing came to mind. I stuck to my friends and family, played ball, and lived my life. Was I perfect? Hell no, but no one could say I'd done anything majorly wrong, besides a few fights here and there—which weren't started by me. People liked to test me, and they ended up finding out that I was more than just a jock who played ball.

"If I did sleep with one of his girls, it shouldn't cause

this many problems. He should be thanking me." I wiggled my brows and they burst into laughter.

"Well, I'm glad you can say that, but I have to deal with the backlash. I think you should put out a statement," Paolo said.

"No."

He groaned and threw his hands up.

"How can I be your agent if you don't listen to me, D?"

"I *do* listen to you."

"60% of the time," Paolo replied.

Reuben and Savion giggled like two little high school kids.

"Which means 60% of the time, you're right," I retorted.

They cackled at my reply. Paolo flipped me off, but he knew I was just kidding. Without him, I wouldn't have been in the best position of my career. Every decision I'd made was alongside him, and I was grateful because I'd just signed a new contract last year for three years at $200M. The endorsement deals were pouring in, and Sutton wanted me to hire an assistant, but I didn't feel like I needed one. She had one, though, so I tended to push everything off on her assistant whenever I could since she was always trying to flirt with me whenever Sutton was not around. She was good at helping me keep on track with everything. Plus, she'd been working with Sutton for the last six months and so far, she'd been on point—besides being a little starstruck at times. I had to remind her that she worked for Sutton, and what she did represented my brand in public.

"Listen to me, Donovan. The only way this can blow over is if you handle it head on," Paolo explained and I grunted, running a hand down my face.

"I need to get to the gym. We have practice tomorrow try not to get into trouble in between time," Savion mentioned, stood, grabbed his stuff, and took it to the trash.

"Let me ride with you." I went to my bedroom and grabbed fresh gym clothes, my cell phone, keys, and wallet.

"Me too and drop me off at my friend's place on the way," Reuben remarked, followed by Savion.

"Donovan, I'm serious. Get with your publicist and come up with something," Paolo continued to complain as he walked out, with us behind him.

I was going to get a little workout in and stop at my parents' house to hang out for a little bit. I slid into the passenger side of Savion's BMW and pushed my seat back, then threw my shades on as the car left the parking structure.

"Normally I agree with you, D. But Paolo might be right about you doing some type of interview to control the narrative." Savion talked over the music.

"Can we have one day without talking about what I need to do for my image?" I muttered, exhausted at the same conversation people kept having about me. Ben will write and talk about me nonstop and nothing I do will change his mind. Savion raised his hand in surrender and my phone buzzed and I lifted it out of my pocket.

"How are you getting to your parents?" Savion changed the subject.

"I'll call a cab to take me there."

"Cool," Savion said.

I have a car at my parents' place in Calabasas that I use whenever I stay. It's my childhood home and I've tried multiple times to get them to move into a bigger place, but they refuse and never let me spoil them. In my father's eyes he loves to keep working at the store, so I stop fighting, besides sending them on trips every year.

"Hello," I answered the call.

"Donovan, why do I have to call you to find out your side of things?" Sutton, my publicist, said.

"What did I do now?" The car pulled in front of the private gym and I got out and grabbed my bag. Reuben took the keys from Savion and backed out of the parking lot, turned and drove off.

"You won't see your car for a few days," I said to him.

"Are you listening to me?" Sutton fussed.

"Sorry, what did you say?"

"Donovan, you pay me a lot of money to keep shit from you. But you're making it harder on me," Sutton responded.

"I'm at the gym, Sutton, sorry I can't hear...Sorry...call." I hung up the call and Savion chortled, and I shrugged. She'll curse me out later so I might as well get a workout in before shit hits the fan even more. We walked through the front entrance of the team's private gym and headed to the locker room and changed clothes.

"You think we got a chance at the ring?" Savion questioned, dumping his bag inside his locker and changing his shirt.

We had a few weeks before the big game, and my nerves were high in anticipation. We were going against our rivals, the New York Stingers, and it would be the most-watched game in history. My rival quarterback, Julian Anderson, was known to talk shit but could barely follow up. That wasn't me being cocky; Julian took the cake as the most egotistical person I'd ever met. Our rivalry went back to us both vying for the position of team captain in college, and a few times, it ended in blows.

"Yep. If we just stay focused, we'll bring another ring home." I shut the locker door and headed out of the room. I went to the weight benches. I lay on my back, adjusted the weights, and started counting in my head.

Savion came in with two towels and bottles of water and stood at the next weight machine. The quietness in the gym helped calm the craziness of the upcoming game, and what I needed to do to get us to the finish line. This would be my second time taking us to the big game in seven years, and I was hopeful to bring the city another win.

"Shit!" Savion blurted out and my eyes popped open.

"What?"

He pointed at the TV screen and I glanced over to see Julian talking with Ben and the message scrolling at the bottom had me ready to kick his ass again. *Donovan Hunt is scared to face me. In college he tried to cheat to win.*

"That motherfucker is lying." I sat up not believing what was happening. I knew Julian and I didn't like each other, but this jackass was trying to take me down.

"Call Sutton so she can get ahead of this, and I'll talk with Coach," Savion said, pulling his phone out of his pocket.

I bent down to grab my phone, and it was already blowing up with missed calls and text messages.

Dad: Call me.

Luna: Donovan call me now. Reporters want a statement.

Paolo: Get your ass on a call now with me.

I closed out of the messages, hit the contact for Sutton, and listened as she picked up on the first ring.

"I already saw it." Sutton blew out a frustrated breath.

"How can he get away with this?"

"You never want to talk, and he got in first. It's a setup, Donovan."

"I've never cheated in my life."

"I know that, but the public doesn't care. It's about the perception." I heard rustling on the other end of the call with Sutton talking to somebody else.

"What's the plan?" I asked, knowing Sutton could fix it

before it went any further. Sutton was the smartest person I knew. She was like a little sister to me, and we constantly butted heads, but she meant well. We'd met through Paolo, when she was looking to start her own business as a publicist and needed clients. Funny, because Savion had a huge crush on her, but she didn't take him seriously when it came to dating; he was like me, and she didn't play about her heart. She and Savion reminded me of the situation with me and Kamara. Both women were beautiful, with their glowing, chestnut skin tone, perfectly arched brows, soft, small hands, and thick, wide curves. The only difference was that I saw Sutton Parks as more of a friend, and nothing sexual.

"I know you won't like this, but I had an idea to do an interview to squash all the nonsense."

"No."

"Donovan you pay me to fix things and this will do that. You need to be open and let people know you're not just the jerk they think you are."

I rubbed the back of my neck.

"Fine, but who am I doing the interview with?"

"I'll let you know later, because you'll fight me on this, and I've had enough of your mouth today." Sutton huffed and ended the call on me like I did earlier.

"She hung up on me."

"My girl," Savion muttered.

"Women," I grumbled, put the phone back on the floor and continued with my workout.

* * *

TWO HOURS later I pulled up to my parents' house in the back of the cab and removed twenty dollars for a tip and shut the door. I headed up the stairs and knocked on the door.

"I wondered how long it would take you to come here," Mom said, moving aside.

I dropped my gym bag and bent down to hug her.

"Ew, you're all sweaty."

I smelled under my arms and chuckled. I planned on showering and eating before I headed home.

"Is Dad here?" I walked toward my old bedroom.

She followed me.

"He's at the shop. Are you hungry? I just made a sandwich and iced tea." She stood at the door as I kicked my shoes off.

"Sure, let me shower really quick."

"Call your sister!" Mom called out as she turned to leave my room.

I shut my door, stripped out of my shorts and shirt, walked into the bathroom, and turned the shower on. It had been a few years since I was back in my old room with all my old posters of athletes that I looked up to growing up, like Michael Jordan, Joe Montana, Muhammad Ali, and John Elway.

I lifted my cell to send a message to my sister.

Me: Sorry, just getting back to you.

Luna: Where are you?

Me: With Mom at the house. I'll call you later.

Luna: All right, love you.

Me: Love you more, bighead.

I placed it back on the counter and opened the shower door. I moved under the water and let it fall down my face and back. I kept thinking about how Sutton needed to turn this around and get Ben off my back before I ended up in jail for beating his ass.

"Kamara!"

I smiled at Rodney as he picked up the cup and wrote down my usual latte. This was my favorite place to hang out when I didn't want to be at home writing or at the office. As a freelance writer, I had to make a way for myself, and many times, I wrote some of my best stories at Cafe Sin. It was a local shop that he started with his sister a few years ago, and they supported a lot of underfunded schools in the city. I wrote a few articles about them, and they ended up taking off and made enough for a second shop in Hollywood.

"Two pumps of vanilla, one espresso, almond milk, extra hot, no foam with vanilla powder on top," Rodney rattled off and I took a sip and moaned. Feeling the coating of the sweet vanilla notes and caffeine kick in were the perfect balance of what I needed today.

"Rodney you're the best." I slid my hand in my purse to pull out money to pay.

"Negative, you don't pay here," Rodney said and tried to push my hand away.

"I'm a customer like anyone else," I argued and tried to put it on the counter but he pushed my hand away.

"Nope. Not on my watch."

"Where's Abigail?" I changed the conversation and eased the money in the tip jar. He still shook his head with a hard grimace. His sister normally worked the front counter of the shop, but I didn't see her today. I glanced around, noticed they changed some of the decor with extra tables and chairs, brighter colors, a section for clothes and products of the brand logo on the front.

"She had to go to the other shop to open up for the manager." Rodney wiped the counter down as I went to the side to not hold up the line.

"Well thank you Rod, let me get out of here and head to the office." I waved at him and sipped on my latte one more time before walking out to my car. I noticed Terry, the homeless guy that stays around the corner from the building. Rodney tried many times to get him to go into a shelter and get help, but he refuses.

"Terry, how are you doing?" I knew people said not to give them money because it only led to drugs, but I wanted to do my part and show him that I was there to support him—no matter what he did with the money I gave him.

"Pretty girl, I'm doing good. I got a hot story for you," he joked, shoving more empty cans in his basket.

That was our thing; every time he saw me, he made up some type of story for me to write up, and I'd sometimes write a fake article with his name as the reporter.

"Really, come on tell me." I went around to the driver's side of my car and put my purse inside and pulled my phone out to take notes.

"I'm your source, right?" he questioned.

"Of course, and if it's really good I'll even see about compensation."

"I like your style, kid," Terry told me.

"Thanks, so who am I writing about now?"

He looked both ways, then stepped closer to the car and dipped his head in the window. I bent down to listen to what he had to say since he was making it seem like it was going to be juicy.

"I think they're trying to buy the block of businesses around here and turn it into a mall."

My brows furrowed in confusion.

"Who's trying to buy the block?"

"The government, I went to the shelter and slept the other night and overheard a conversation."

"Maybe you misunderstood, Terry. That doesn't sound right."

Terry shrugged his shoulders.

"I could be wrong, but your friends in the coffee shop were arguing about it earlier today," Terry commented.

I looked back at the coffee shop, biting my bottom lip nervously. Hopefully, Terry was wrong about that, but I'd keep my eyes and ears open. I normally got alerts from the local City Council about upcoming elections.

"Thanks for the tip, Terry. I need to get to work." I leaned over and passed him a ten-dollar bill and he grinned.

"Go eat real food please."

"Thanks, pretty girl." Terry tapped the hood of my car.

I put the key in, started the ignition, and slid my seatbelt on. I watched through the back window as I drove into traffic, seeing Terry talking to another homeless man and showing him the money that I gave him. I changed lanes and got in the left turn lane.

Working at the local paper with my best friend was great when we wanted to have lunch together. Our other best friend, Sutton, worked as a publicist for some of the biggest stars and athletes, but she was still humble and sweet and never let it go to her head. Luna and I met Sutton when she came onboard as Donovan's publicist a few years ago. Meeting the two of them forced me to come out of my shell and relax.

Growing up, I'd focused more on getting to the next big thing, rather than living in the moment. My parents supported everything I wanted to do—even pursuing a journalism career. It was funny; in high school I was on the debate team, ran for class president, and tried to get the students to push their parents to vote for a new principal. It didn't work, and I ended up getting detention for constantly speaking about things that a child shouldn't speak about. Cheryl and William Powell had raised me to speak my mind and call out something if I felt it was wrong. My mom worked as a dentist, and my dad was a retired army veteran who started his own nonprofit to support other veterans. I'd tried many times to get Terry to speak with my dad, but he always had an excuse.

At twenty-eight, I had everything I'd ever wanted out of life, from my career to my apartment, family, and friends. The only thing I was really missing was love—something I kept failing at, based on my background with men. Somehow, I kept finding frogs that made promises to love and protect me like a princess, but they tended to either cheat, stomp on my career, or only take what they could get once they found out that I knew Donovan Hunt.

"Ugh," I groaned, thinking of Donovan.

I told Luna all the time that she was related to someone who only cared about himself, and the women who fell all over him had no self-respect. Was he handsome? Yes. I mean, he was 6'3" with a chiseled jawline, broad shoulders, an eight-pack stomach, and heart-shaped, full lips that I always stared at whenever we were in the same room together. Don't get me started on his oceanic, green-blue eyes that sometimes left me speechless.

"Stop it," I mumbled to myself, trying to shake off the thoughts of Donovan. I'd known him since I was nineteen years old, a freshman in college, back when Luna and I were roommates, and best friends since the first day we met.

I finally arrived at work and parked in the employee area. I turned the car off and grabbed my things. The *Los Angeles Life* newspaper had been my home for the last three years after they recruited me from my blog posts. Luna followed me, and when they saw her fashion style and pics, it really made her social media a hit. She and I had offices across from each other, and she tended to get there late, so I wouldn't have been surprised if she was working from home that day.

I waved at the receptionist and walked down the hall of the red brick building to my office. The daily news stories seemed to be causing everyone in the building to have high anxiety.

"Finally, you're here." Cailey, the senior editor, caught me as I opened my office door.

I dropped my bag on the couch, sat in my chair, and placed my coffee down, then turned on my computer. "Hello, Cailey."

She hated when I did that. Everyone knew me long enough that if you didn't say hello first, I wouldn't continue a conversation. It's rude off the bat to demand something when you haven't even acknowledged my presence.

"Hello Kamara." Cailey cocked her head to the side standing in the middle of my office.

"What can I do for you? You seem stressed."

"Aren't I always?"

"That's true." I typed in my password and pulled up my list of potential stories I wanted to cover for the next post.

"I have a story for you," Cailey said.

"Cool, email it to me."

"I normally would, but this is a special case."

"What do you mean?"

I pulled the drawer open and grabbed my glasses to start my research.

"I got you an exclusive story," Cailey said.

I noticed her hands were behind her back.

"Okay. About the mayor? Governor?"

She brought her hand from around her back and placed the magazine down on my desk with Donovan Hunt circled in a red pen.

"No." I pushed the sports magazine away from me.

"Yes."

"No, I do public policy pieces. Things that make a difference."

"This makes a difference and sports is important," Cailey argued.

I leaned back in the chair and pinched the bridge of my nose.

"Cailey, you have plenty of people here that can do the interview."

"That person is you. This is perfect, you're already friends with him."

"I'm friends with his sister. Donovan and I are associates."

I couldn't blurt out that once or twice I had a wet dream about him, but that was because I accidently walked in on him when he was naked from the shower.

"You're doing the interview. Sorry, it's final."

"That's not fair, Cailey. You promised when I came here

that I could create my own lane." I jumped up, crossing my arms over my chest.

"Which I have held up on my end. This is one story with a photoshoot," Cailey muttered lowly and my eyes grew wide in surprise.

"Hold up, back up. Photoshoot? Is this a magazine or newspaper company?" I needed to find someone else to take this project from me.

"Newspaper. This would be good for your career. Change it up for once; maybe he'll surprise you."

I smacked my teeth.

"Yeah right."

"Listen it's a done deal and Sutton will contact you about the details."

"Wait, so this is Sutton's idea?" I wondered if my best friend was behind this. It must be important.

"Yep, she called me and asked if you could do the story."

"When is this happening?"

"In three days," Cailey mumbled and my head jerked back.

"Three days?! You just gave me the information today. I can't be prepared that fast."

She shrugged her shoulders.

"You got this Kamara, stop stressing and call Sutton," Cailey called out as she turned and walked out.

I picked up my desk phone and dialed Sutton's numbers as I scanned the magazine that Cailey left in my office. *Superstar athlete. Yeah right.*

"Hello," Sutton answered.

"Really Sutton?"

"I knew you'd be the right person because you're unbiased and would give him a fair shot."

"Ugh, I write about the issues with rundown tenant buildings, not who's catching a football."

"Think of it like a public policy issue."

"Please tell me how me writing a puff piece on him is helping the public?" I questioned.

"I knew you would be enthusiastic about this," Sutton sarcastically threw in my face.

"You owe me."

"Drinks on me."

"Drinks, dinner, and whatever else I want for a week."

"A week!" she screeched through the phone.

"Fine two days of you buying lunch."

"That's better, but I'll still do drinks and dinner. Call Luna and see what she's doing later," Sutton replied.

I made a mental note to text Luna after I finished the call.

"So, this is happening here at the office, right?"

"No, I booked a photoshoot and want you to come down and talk to him there," Sutton explained.

"Where?"

The phone went silent and I knew she was keeping something else from me.

"Don't be annoyed, but his place."

"Suttonnnn…" I whined, not in the mood to be driving all the way across town, dealing with traffic, and his team that probably won't give me the space to answer my questions.

"I promise you won't have any problems and he'll be ready for you," Sutton said.

"I need to get to work, you owe me big time and I want a huge slice of chocolate cake for dinner."

She chuckled at my request and said okay.

"Thank you, best friend. See you tonight."

We both hung the phone up and I walked around my desk, grabbed my cell out of my purse and texted Luna.

Me: Dinner tonight?

Luna: I was just thinking this.
Me: Sutton's paying.
Sutton: Don't get too crazy now.
Luna: Oops. What did you do, Sutton?
Sutton: Nothing.
Me: Don't lie.
Sutton: Get to work and talk later.
Luna: I just got to the office.

I looked up and saw Luna waving at another coworker as she strolled to my office.

Me: An hour late.
Luna: I needed to meditate.
Sutton: LOL! Translation means "get your morning orgasm from some guy".
Luna: No comment.

I shook my head and dropped my phone on the desk as she smiled, put her phone away, and sauntered in my office.

"You look chipper," Luna commented.

"You look flushed," I teased and she waved me off.

"Sutton tell you about the interview?"

I narrowed my eyes.

"Am I the last person to know about this?"

"Probably, but it'll be fine. My brother needs this more than you do," Luna said and that gave me pause.

"What are you talking about?"

"Ben Simmons had Julian Anderson on his show, and they made some stupid allegations about my brother."

"Oh. I haven't watched any TV or been on social media today."

She released a breath.

"Yeah, it's all over the blogs and airing on FSGN on repeat. Sutton thought it would be good to do an interview and I agreed with her about you doing it since you barely talk to him."

"I talk to him."

Luna gave me that bitch please look.

"'Talk' and 'like' are two different things and since you're not his biggest fan, no one will fault you for the interview," Luna explained. It made sense. All I wrote about was how corrupt things were, and not so much about celebrity and athlete gossip. I couldn't even say what year he'd won his big game ring.

"Let me get to work before Cailey comes looking for me." Luna stood and I nodded.

"Luna."

"Yeah."

"You might want to put a bra on. Someone is probably going to be calling you soon to bring you the one you just left at their place," I said.

Her phone started ringing, and I shook my head. She dropped her head in embarrassment.

For the rest of the day, I'd gone through footage of Donovan playing games and read up on his stats as a quarterback with the team. As soon as six o'clock hit, I finished for the day, drove home, showered, and changed to get to the restaurant by 7:30 for dinner. D'Andrea's Restaurant was crowded but luckily enough, Sutton had called ahead and reserved a table for three.

Luna was busy texting on her phone, as the waitress came over to greet us and drop off the menus.

"Our specials for today are linguini and meatballs."

"I want a large bowl of the mushroom risotto," Luna announced.

"Can I get pasta con pomodoro e basilico?" I asked the waitress.

"Good choice," Meredith responded, writing our orders down.

"They both sound good, but I'll be different with spaghetti alle vongole," Sutton said.

"What would you ladies like to drink?" Meredith questioned, taking our menus off the table.

"Red wine please," Sutton replied.

"You're fine with the appetizer of bruschetta?" Meredith wondered and we all nodded.

Luna finally placed her phone down and we all looked at each other and then burst into laughter.

"I can't begin to tell you how embarrassed I was this morning," Luna said, grabbing the dessert menu off the table and fanning herself.

"Who's the guy?" I asked.

"It's a friend."

"Luna Hunt. Are you keeping a secret from your best friends?" I pointed between me and Sutton.

"Sounds like she is," Sutton backed me up.

"You guys I like him, but I know once it gets out everything might change," Luna explained.

"Is he keeping you a secret?" I questioned, not liking my friend being someone's little side piece.

"No, it's my choice. He's well-known," Luna said.

Meredith strolled back to the table with a bottle of red wine and a plate of appetizers with a side salad, and smaller plates for us to split everything.

"I'm starving." I helped pass the plates around the table as Sutton opened the bottle to pour wine into our glasses.

"Dinner will be out shortly," Meredith announced, leaving more napkins on the table.

"So, what about your love life, Sutton? I can't be the only one getting some pleasure." Luna drank from her glass and smacked her lips loudly.

"Unfortunately, the men department is very thin on my end. I've been ending up with little boys that ask me out on dates, and I end up paying or they live with their momma or roommate." Sutton rolled her eyes then picked up the fork to eat her salad. They both glanced over at me.

"What?" I bit into the bruschetta.

"Who are you seeing right now?" Luna asked.

"Nobody."

"Mmm," Luna responded.

"Unlike you Luna I have too much work to juggle. Dating can wait."

"Nothing wrong with a casual thing here and there. Dip and dabble," Sutton implied, dipping the bread in the olive oil and sauce.

"When's the last time you've had sex?" Luna asked.

"I don't know and let's talk about something else."

"Come on you remember, six months?"

I shook my head no.

"Nine months?" Sutton asked.

I lowered my eyes avoiding their stares.

"A year?" Luna whispered and I rubbed my temples and blew out a breath.

"Bitch! Are you a virgin?" Sutton blurted out and I covered her mouth with my hand, and she smacked it away.

"No! OMG you two are the worst."

"So, what's the big deal? Just tell us," Luna said.

"Fine, three years," I mumbled under my breath.

Their eyes ballooned.

"Damn, do you have a toy at least?" Sutton replied, and I rubbed the back of my neck nervously.

Luna choked on her wine and I jumped up and patted her back.

"I'm okay... fine."

The entire restaurant looked over at us.

This was so embarrassing.

"Do you need help with anything?" Meredith asked.

"I mean if the dinner could come with a side of a big, long-" Luna started to say, and I glared at her.

"No, we're fine, thank you," Luna responded.

"Sure. I'll give you a few more minutes before I refill your wine," Meredith explained, then went back to the kitchen.

"How is it possible to go three years without any type of sex?" Sutton said.

"I just haven't found anyone that appeals to me."

"Girl, a blow-up doll would appeal to me in that amount of time without sex," Luna joked and I flipped her off.

"You two need to stop acting like your sex lives are all that. You both just started getting laid might I add."

"Honey, even if I didn't have a man, I'd still use my hand," Sutton said, waving her hand in my face.

"Anyway, let's rein it in and focus. So, how are things with the business?" I asked Sutton, steering the conversation away from my lack of a love life. I honestly was too caught up with building my career to even notice the last time a man touched me. Thinking back, the last guy I went out with had to have been Lex, whom I met at a grocery store one day. He was grabbing something for his mom, and I was looking less than stellar, but he found me attractive and asked me out. We went out on a few dates, but all he did was talk about himself, and how much money he had. It was a big turn-off, and a waste of time… but he did have a mean tongue game.

"What are you thinking about to have you smiling like that?" Luna waved a napkin in my face.

"Nothing important."

"Mmm-hmm," Luna responded.

"The business is good; clients are happy, and I'm making money," Sutton said as Meredith placed our food on the table.

"This looks delicious," I said.

"Enjoy, ladies, and please let me know if you need

anything else," Meredith said, taking our leftover dishes away.

I dove into my meal and moaned at the first taste.

"If only a man was giving you that satisfaction," Luna joked.

I stuck my tongue out at her, and we all burst into laughter. The entire evening was filled with laughter, wine, and great food. We stayed there for another hour before finally going our separate ways.

I made it back home, unlocked my apartment door, and sighed. The place wasn't too messy from earlier. Whenever I got into a story, I tended to focus just on that, and my cleaning tended to get pushed aside. Strolling into the kitchen, I opened the fridge to get a bottle of water before checking my voice messages.

"Kamara, it's your mom. I want to have lunch and go shopping this weekend call me back."

Every other Saturday it's girls' day and we get our nails and hair done and lunch together while my father goes fishing with his friends. I'll more than likely have to check my calendar especially with this interview coming up.

"Calling for a Kamara Powell, we'd love to have you come down and discuss your piece on environmental hazards at News channel three."

"Interesting."

I continued to listen to each message when the last one had me stuck in place.

"Kamara, this is D. Well, Donovan Hunt. I just heard you're doing the interview with me, and I wanted to make sure that you can keep it professional. You know, being my sister's best friend, and all." He cleared his throat.

I grew hot all over. For him to have the audacity to call and try to check me about being professional. Him, of all people! He got the right person today. I picked up the phone and redialed since he was the last number to call.

"Hello." I heard a deep, groggy voice.

"What the hell do you mean be professional!"

"Who is this?" he asked.

"Answer the question."

"Listen, it's late, and I'm not sure who you are, or when we slept together, but I'm not interested," he replied.

I felt offended by his choice of words. *Is this how he does every girl he comes into contact with?*

"It's Kamara, jackass," I spat back.

I heard him groan, and it sounded like he was moving around in bed. "Kamara, I have early practice tomorrow. Are you drunk?"

"What! No, I mean I had a few drinks tonight at dinner. But I'm perfectly coherent."

"Who did you go to dinner with?" he asked.

"Why?"

"Because I want to know."

"That's none of your business."

"Says who?"

I was getting frustrated by this entire conversation and a little flustered.

"Listen, my dinner dates are none of your business. I'm just returning your call from earlier."

"What did you wear? I hope it was appropriate," Donovan grunted and I wondered what the meaning behind the attitude was.

"Since when do you care about what is appropriate? The little football bimbos I see hanging around you sure aren't dressed like they're going to church," I replied annoyed, and sat on the edge of my bed, and removed my heels.

"Ugh," I grunted, massaging my feet from being in heels so long today.

"What's that noise?" he asked.

"Listen. I just wanted to let you know this wasn't by choice doing this interview with you." I closed my eyes, yawned, and pushed myself up against the headboard.

"Am I keeping you up past your bedtime?" he joked.

"No, I just had too much to drink tonight."

"Who was the date with?"

"I... The date is none of your business. Just be ready for the interview please."

"Are you rushing me off the phone? Is he there with you?"

"What? No and why do you care?" I huffed, checking the time on the nightstand for my wakeup time. Something about the change in his voice wanted me to confess who I was with, at the same time he is my best friend's brother. Our paths and friends are so different.

"I don't since you woke me up. Thought I'd return the favor."

"Okay D. Thanks for letting me know about the interview."

"Donovan."

"Huh?"

"Call me 'Donovan'."

"Everyone calls you D."

"You're not everyone," he replied and the tension through the phone could be cut with a knife.

"Okay. What about bighead? Can I call you that?" I joked, trying to break up the moment.

"Only if you're talking about the head below," he responded, and my mouth dropped open in shock.

"Um, I need to go," I said and rushed to end the call. I flopped headfirst on the mattress and screamed. *Was*

Donovan flirting with me? He'd always been a jackass and a prankster. Maybe I was reading into things. I turned over and rose, then headed into the bathroom to shower before I got some sleep. I still needed to look into the details of the City Council, plus prepare for the interview with Donovan.

*T*wo days later, Sutton asked me to come into her office to sign off on a few things, so my items could be donated to charity events. We also had to figure out the interview with *Los Angeles Life*. When Sutton called and said Kamara was conducting the interview, at first I was shocked because she'd always been more of an activist type of journalist. Her agreeing to do a sports story seemed weird. But knowing I would get to see her again and push her buttons made it even more fun.

Sutton's office was in Century City, not far from my place, so I decided to stop at one of my favorite coffee shops before making it to her place. I opened the door, removed my shades, and looked to see if my favorite girl was working today. Abigail and her brother had started Cafe Sin. This was their second location, and the one closest to me.

I stood in line, slid one hand in my pocket, and texted with the other, while I waited for the customer ahead of me to finish ordering.

Reuben: Club tomorrow night?

Savion: Coach said practice tomorrow.

Reuben could go out and stay out all night and still get up for practice with lots of energy. Me, I needed loads of caffeine to stay awake. Plus, the women don't understand about keeping their distance when we want to just chill and not be bothered.

Me: I'll pass.

Reuben: Stop being a pussy.

Me: Fuck you.

Savion: Reuben, you'll just end up in a hotel and bail on us.

Reuben: What's wrong with that?

"Hello, handsome."

I lifted my head, hearing an angelic voice.

"Abigail, you're looking lovely today. Did you dress up for me?"

She rolled her eyes.

"That's your problem. A big ass flirt, D."

"Aww, Abigail you wound me. You know I only have eyes for you."

Abigail smacked her teeth and waved me off.

"There are two people you can't lie to, sir: me and God. I see through those green-blue eyes." Abigail picked up a cup and started writing my normal drink down.

I started to pull out my money.

"See that's why it will never work. You're cold, woman."

I pulled a twenty dollar bill out to pay and she smacked my hand away.

"You know I don't take your money."

"If Rodney was here, he'd take it."

"Probably, but you help us a lot when you post about us. Anyway, how are you doing?" Abigail walked over to the coffee machine and started making an espresso caramel latte.

I stood in front of the machine and continued to talk

and look around the shop. I'd met her and her brother through my sister, after she told me about them. I decided to try the place for myself, and the first person who called me out on my shit was Abigail, when I tried to skip the line. We'd been friends ever since.

"I'm betting on you guys. Make sure you bring the trophy home." Abigail poured the milk inside, grabbed the lid and passed it over to me.

"How much?"

"A hundred."

"That's all I'm worth to you, Abigail?"

"You don't want the answer to that, buddy." We both burst into laughter.

"Fine, let me get out of here and get ready for Sutton to bust my balls."

"Oh, that reminds me." Abigail passed another latte over to me.

"When did I become her errand boy?"

"Stop being an ass, D. Not sure what type of woman puts up with you, but she's not doing her job right."

"Babe, the position's open. Think about it." I slid my shades back on and started to walk out of the shop.

I heard Abigail call out to me teasingly, "Sorry, babe! I like my coffee dark, no cream or sugar!"

I chuckled, shaking my head at her.

"Cream can be fulfilling." Abigail was one of those chicks I could hang out with—like Sutton—and be completely platonic.

I slid the key in the door, started the ignition, and drove off toward Sutton's office with her drink in my hand. Kaci was already there, according to Sutton's last message—which reminded me that I forgot to respond to Reuben about tomorrow night. I fished my cell out of my pocket as I drove.

Reuben: Did he leave us on read?

Savion: Probably.

Me: My bad. I was talking to Abigail and now heading to Sutton.

Reuben: Tell Abigail I'm still waiting.

Me: Reuben, I like Abigail too much to make her suffer by hooking her up with you.

Reuben: Stop hating on me.

Me: Might have better luck with Sutton.

Savion: Naw, keep her name out of this conversation.

I almost spit my coffee out at Savion's response about Sutton.

Reuben: Savion, you can't handle competition?

Savion: Reuben, we're boys, but Sutton's mine.

Reuben: Does she know that?

Savion: She will once I get my lips between something sweet.

Me:. I don't want to hear that shit about Sutton.

Reuben: She's free rein.

I turned right at the light on Century Park and pulled up to valet. I parked with the car still running. I hopped out and left him with the car, then walked inside the building and nodded at the front staff. She was in the same building as Paolo's agency, so it was easier when I needed to have meetings with them about my career.

Me: About to head into the meeting.

Savion: Cool. What about the club?

Reuben: What about me and Sutton?

Savion: Reuben, don't get fucked up.

Me: You two idiots work this out on your own. I'm getting on the elevator.

I closed out of the message thread and put my phone away, tapped the fifth floor and sipped on the rest of my coffee. A minute later the doors opened, and I stepped out grinning wide at the person sitting at the front desk.

"Now, aren't you too pretty to be working out front?" I asked, sitting on the edge of Margaret's desk. She was Sutton's aunt. She was in her late 60s, and she was hired to help out. She seemed to fit in with everyone, and I found out really quickly where Sutton got her spunk.

"Mr. Hunt, I suggest you get your butt off my desk before I put a newspaper to your bottom."

"Margaret, I thought we go way back."

"Those eyes won't win me over. Now, I see you listened to me and made the play to get ahead of your win," Margaret said.

I smirked. She would always tell me when I messed up on a play—and even sent messages through Sutton when we won. I didn't have any close older relatives besides my parents, who didn't want anything from me. Margaret could still pass for being in her early 40s, with her wrinkle-free, dark brown skin, and long, curly silver hair.

"What makes you think I used your advice?" I egged on. She blew out a breath and motioned for me to come closer to hear.

"You're so happy and I know it's not about a girl."

"I'm waiting for you, beautiful."

"Boy, I'll hurt you."

"I like hurt. Besides, I can handle you." I winked and stood laughing at her pursed lips.

"Don't let the age fool you, son. I still get the gentleman callers," Margaret told me and I played along with a hard glare.

"I'm telling, Sutton. Your supposed to wait for me."

"Baby you couldn't handle me back then or now. But you can get me tickets to a game." Margaret grinned then pointed at her cheek.

"Fine, but one day Margaret, I get you on my side." I bent down and kissed her cheek.

"Stop flirting with my auntie D and get in here," Sutton called out.

I headed inside and saw Kaci sitting on the couch wearing a short black dress, which ran up her thigh. Her blond hair was pulled up in a high bun on top of her head and the pink blouse was slightly open showing her cleavage. Sutton must have told her I was coming in too and she dressed up. I chuckled to myself.

"What's funny?" Sutton asked. I passed her the drink that Abigail made for her earlier.

"Nothing, just thinking."

Sutton sipped on her drink and I sat in the chair in front of her desk, kicked my feet up on her desk and as usual she smacked them down.

"Sutton, isn't the saying, 'customers are always right'?"

"Probably in some areas, not in my office."

"Hi, Donovan," Kaci said.

I turned my head and nodded. "It's D."

"Be nice, jackass," Sutton said.

"What'd I do?" I shrugged my shoulders.

Sutton rubbed her temples.

"Anyway. Kaci and I have the photoshoot and interview ready for you. I need you on your best behavior."

"I'm always on my best behavior."

"I need your one hundred percent, chipper, sweet behavior that you give the kids."

"For an interview, come on now, Sutton. You're pushing it now."

She pointed her pen in my direction.

"No, you come on. I refuse to have this mess up Mara's opportunity." Sutton's brow raised in question.

"I thought this was about me." I leaned up with my hands clasped together.

"It is, but you need to be open with her and not diffi-cult. This can be good for both of you," Sutton explained.

"Does she know to be nice to me?"

"I'm not going there with you. Check these out and let me know what you think. I can have a stylist brings them over to you," Sutton said.

"I thought you worked for me," I fussed and Sutton sat back in her seat and stared at me.

I raised my hands in surrender knowing what was going to come out of her mouth.

"You can act all macho with your little friends, and Margaret, but watch your cockiness with me."

"Savion must have not called you," I joked and she tried to reach over and grab me, and I jumped up fast out of her reach laughing.

"Fuck you, D," Sutton said.

"Why is everybody saying that to me?" I placed my hands on my hips, looking behind me toward Kaci and back at Sutton. A few seconds go by and all three of us laugh.

"OMG, I swear you get on my nerves," Sutton said.

"You know you love me. Come on, bring it to Daddy." I held my arms out for a hug and walked toward her.

Her hand went out, stopping me. "Sit your butt down and go through what we have. Kaci, tell him about the charity items," Sutton said.

"Sure. Um, I was speaking with Sutton and we came up with five items to have you sign." Kaci stood and switched over to me, holding out her iPad. I looked down and saw she had a list with the game winning ball signed uniform, pants, shoes, and football card.

"I'm fine with the ball, shoes, shirt, and card. The pants don't need to be in a charity for kids."

"But it would bring in the most money," Kaci said.

"I doubt any of the kids would want my sweaty pants in their face."

"It's fine Kaci we can get a hat signed," Sutton remarked and Kaci went to sit back down.

"Anything else I need to know about?"

"Try to not be in the clubs with multiple women if possible. I've gotten photos of you drunk out with your friends."

"I can't promise that, Sutton. We just won the Championship title."

"Exactly and the big game is right around the corner," Sutton blurted out, tapping on her keyboard.

A few times the press caught wind of me out drunk and now that's the main headline. Coming into the game after college and making a name for myself was beyond my wildest dreams and did I get a little cocky and reckless? Sometimes, but at thirty-two I've slowed down in my view. Mostly the weekends are when I tend to let loose and not every day like Reuben's ass.

I slide a hand down my face.

"I can promise I will be more aware and not end up on any blogs." I held my hand out to shake on my promise.

"If you fail. What do I get?"

"A date with Reuben."

"Get out of my office and email Kaci after you approve those outfits, please." Sutton pushed me away from her desk.

I cackled, grabbing the pictures off her desk, blowing her a kiss, and leaving.

"Keep that armed iced up!" Margaret called out.

"Yes ma'am."

I always had a good time whenever I came to pick on Sutton and Margaret at the office, either by aggravating them with my charm, being defiant about going somewhere, or faking like I liked someone who they wanted me to meet.

I waited for the elevator to ding, and the doors opened. I stepped on to go to Paolo's office. Before I left the other day, I never finished our conversation since I had to go to the gym. So, I figured I'd drop in now while I was in the building, before I went to see my parents and study some footage.

I got off on the 10th floor a few minutes later and saw the hustle and bustle of the office, as people roamed around like chickens with their heads cut off. I wondered if it had anything to do with me. I knocked on Paolo's door. He was sitting in his chair with his phone to his ear. He waved for me to step in. I looked around, not remembering when he had put in the 60-inch TV, black lounge chair, and bar in the corner.

"What brings you over?" Paolo asked, extending a hand for me to shake.

"I was with Sutton talking about the interview. When did you get this stuff?" I pointed to the chair, TV, and bar.

"Called having rich clients," Paolo said.

"That fifteen percent is getting cut. Remind me to talk to my accountant."

"Nope. Take a seat." Paolo sat and entwined his hands on the desk.

"How much do you think this interview will help?" I wanted to be sure I wasn't putting myself out there to make Ben look good and show he finally won and got me out of my comfort zone.

"Honestly, you could probably do without the interview."

"So why am I doing it then!"

"Because you're all over the place, D. I love you like a brother, but you need to cut the shit."

"You act like you're not with us sometimes."

"Keyword, sometimes. You let Reuben drag you into stupid shit," Paolo said, and that reminded me of the time Reuben had us judging a wet t-shirt contest and the prize was a kiss from all three of us.

"He can be a little reckless."

Paolo looked at me straight, deadpan like you're being an idiot for no reason.

"I love Reuben, but he needs to slow down before he ends up with three baby mommas and naked in a hotel room," Paolo replied, turned his computer to me and showed me the latest BTZ gossip blog headline; Reuben with bloodshot red eyes and his shirt off in front of a club.

"I'll talk to him."

"Good, but the interview could be beneficial. You're not getting younger, Donovan; you need something that shows you're more than just a football player. Show the world the stuff you do behind the scenes," Paolo explained.

I had done charity work and helped build homes for Habitat for Humanity during my off-season.

"All right, let me get out of here. I'm supposed to go see my parents and then study up on some footage before the big game."

"Sounds good."

We shook hands again. I strolled out of his office and back to the valet. I grabbed my keys and went across town to visit my parents before I headed home to work.

I pushed the key into the lock, hearing laughter from the other side of the door. I opened the door, surprised to see my sister there on a workday afternoon. My dad was sitting in his armchair with his beer, and Mom wasn't nearby. But surprisingly, another guest was sitting in the place where my mom usually sat when she watched TV.

"Hey D." Luna jumped up and ran toward me to give me a hug and kiss. I bear hugged her and kissed her cheek, while staring back at Kamara as she looked down at her cell phone typing. I wanted to know who she was talking to that had her attention away from me.

"Son, what are you doing here?" Dad said.

"I was in the neighborhood." I shut the door and went further in the living room.

"Who's at the door?" My mom sauntered in with her usual white apron on and a towel in her hand.

"Just me, your favorite." I grinned, picking her up and kissing her on the forehead.

"Boy hush with the lies," Mom replied.

"It's okay Mom, we can tell Luna now about being adopted."

Luna punched me in the arm, and I ran behind Mom to get away.

"You two stop it right now."

"He started it though," Luna whined, trying to run behind the other side of the couch.

"Lloyd, come and get your son," Mom said.

"Leave your sister alone, Donovan."

I pinched her on the arm and she smacked my hand, and I rubbed the sting away. I went around the couch and plopped down next to Kamara and stretched my arm on the back of the chair. I cocked my head to the side and licked my lips.

"You can't speak?"

"D. Leave me alone." She continued typing away on her cell.

I snatched the phone from her hand and looked through the thread. She gasped and lunged at my arm, trying to get it back. Her shirt rode up, and I saw a small mole on her lower stomach. She caught me staring at her stomach, and she shoved her shirt down. I gripped her waist gently.

"Donovan, give her phone back and stop being rude!" Mom yelled.

As Kamara and I locked eyes, I felt like we were the only ones in the room.

"Can I have my phone, please?" she asked.

"What do I get out of it?"

"You get to keep your fingers," she said snarkily with a smile.

I raised the phone higher away from her. The room was

large enough that no one could see what I was doing as I ran a hand up and down Kamara's hip.

"That's not nice. Aren't you supposed to be all about love and peace in the world?" I did air quotes with one hand.

She tried to move out of my hold, but that only made my dick even harder and poke at her stomach. She gasped, tried to wiggle out of my hold and I smirked.

"Keep moving like that and he'll wake up," I whispered in her ear.

"Give me that." Luna grabbed the phone out of my hand, and I laughed letting Kamara up out of my hold.

"Who's Terry?"

I saw the name being mentioned between her and Rodney from Cafe Sin and wondered if he was her boyfriend.

"None of your business," Mara said, as she tried to avoid eye contact. I glanced at the clock on the wall and back down to Mara and grinned.

"Kam, ignore my stupid brother. He's just mad the only girls that want him are the dumb bimbos," Luna told her and I flipped her off behind my Dad's back.

"Daddy, Donovan just flipped me off," Luna snitched on me, then ran back to the kitchen with my mom.

My dad was stuck in his own world, with the TV blasting the highlights from my game.

"I hope your boyfriend doesn't get jealous."

"I don't-" she started to answer, but stopped, realizing I was trying to dig into her love life.

"You don't what?"

"I need to get going." Mara pulled herself up off me and I sat up watching as she gathered her things to leave.

"Luna I'll see you later," Mara called out, walked over to my Dad, and kissed him on the cheek.

"What about me?"

"What about you?"

"I don't get a kiss on the cheek?"

Dad laughed. I glared at him.

"I like your dad," Mara said and everybody started laughing at my expense.

"Call me later, girl." Luna walked her out to her car and shut the front door. I jumped up and went into the kitchen to bug my mom.

"Women," I mumbled to myself.

Mom was opening the stove and putting a tray of biscuits in. She started to cut some vegetables.

I sauntered over and picked up a carrot, then lifted myself onto the counter.

"If you like her, then I suggest you stop with the other floosies in your life," Mom said, chopping onions.

"She's different from what I'm used to."

"You mean a woman with a brain."

"She might not fit in my world."

"According to who?" Mom swung her gaze toward me. I titled my head. She knew what I was talking about. "Kamara is an intelligent, beautiful, and kind person. I don't see the problem with that."

"I know that, but she's always trying to fight something because that puts her in the middle of drama and then to top it off media pressure."

"When have you ever let media pressure dictate your choices?"

"I'd rather not have her see the ugliness of that part. I deal with it enough and the judgment and name calling."

"Well, it's up to you how you want to handle things."

My family knew I'd had a crush on Kamara since the first time I met her, and they thought she was too good for me. She was smart, beautiful, and knew what she wanted out of life—and it didn't hurt that her body was out of this world, but she was always modest in the clothes she wore. I wondered if she knew how many men stared at her—even when she just wore tights and a big t-shirt. No matter what, her voluptuous tits and wide hips would be on display. She was toned but curvy, with meat on her bones —thick in all the right places.

"Are you listening to me?" Mom asked.

"I'm sorry, what did you say?" I couldn't tell her I'd gotten distracted thinking about Kamara's ass and breasts.

"I said, 'Focus on the game coming up and let everything else fall into place,'" she said and tossed the vegetables in the pot.

I hopped down and kissed the top of her head, then walked back out to the living room with my dad. We watched the rest of the game until dinner was ready.

ONCE DINNER WAS OVER, I went out to the bar to meet up with Savion for drinks. Still full of dinner at my folks' place I was just looking to release some energy and possibly find someone to bring home. Unfortunately, the women in the bar were too thirsty and wasted so I passed and continued ordering shots.

"What happened with Reuben?"

Savion gave the waitress his empty beer bottle and she replied with a fresh new one. Bar Cutz was a bar that all the high-profile people came to to get away from the lights and cameras. But it ended up making the place even more famous so we really couldn't hide out anymore. A few girls danced together on the floor.

"He got held up with somebody. He was all secretive

and shit," Savion mentioned and that sounded like Reuben's ass.

"Hopefully, he doesn't have another pregnancy scare."

"Yeah, I keep telling him these women are only using him."

"I saw Sutton today." I watched his eyes move from the women dancing on the floor back to me.

"How is she?"

"Fine I guess."

"She doesn't take me seriously."

"Can you blame her?" I asked.

He gave me a hard grimace.

"You're the last person to talk about anyone's reputation."

"Yo, never said I was perfect, bro. Sutton is different."

"I know Sutton's more than a piece of meat. I know I joke around with Reuben and you, but I care about her."

"I think she likes you, but she says the lifestyle of a pro athlete and the female fans don't make it easy."

"Enough about me, what's up with you."

"I have to do this interview with Kamara."

"Luna's friend Kamara?"

I glance over my shoulder hearing the commotion of two guys fighting over some woman.

"Yep."

"I thought she wrote stuff about saving the ocean or something."

I chortled at his statement.

"She does. Well, it's mostly like keeping the city updated on what's happening. I guess Sutton asked her to do this for her."

"Kamara's cool."

"Yeah." I motioned for the waitress to bring me another beer.

"You like her don't you?" He plastered a big smile on his face.

"What! No she's Luna's friend."

He smirked, as the waitress came back to the table with fresh beers and shots for us. I pulled a fifty dollar bill out of my pocket and put it in the pocket of her shorts. She wore a crop top and shorts.

"Keep it real, D. You have the same problems as me with Sutton."

"You're tripping."

"Whatever you say."

I was no longer interested in this conversation. I wanted to get up and leave for the night. Hearing Kamara's name on another guy's lips—even if he was a friend of mine—caused a tightness in my chest.

"I have to get out of here. We have footage to look over, and practice tomorrow, plus I need to get ready for the interview." I rose out of the booth and felt a pair of hands around my waist. I looked down at the tiny hands, then over my shoulder in shock.

"Miss me?" Tabitha tried to kiss me on the lips, and I turned my head and removed her hands from around my waist.

"What are you doing here?"

"You don't look happy to see me, big fella." She ran her index finger down my chest to the top of my belt buckle.

I stepped out of her hold.

"Tabitha, let's not act like this was more than a hookup."

She rolled her eyes, and she stepped further into my personal space.

"You remember how I used to make you feel?" she questioned.

I was trying to not be a jerk and spill all her business in front of everyone. But she was pushing me in that direction. I scratched the back of my neck and sighed in annoyance. Tabitha wanted more from our hookups, but she didn't think to try and get to know me beyond football and all of our conversations were mostly about her and what she wanted to do in life.

"I need to get going."

"I'll see you around, baby." Tabitha winked and swished her hips trying to get my attention. She was sexy, I'll give her that much, but personality wise it was a dumpster fire.

"Tabby is back." Savion shook his head. I shrugged, not caring if she was. I'd never step backwards and hook up with her again. I know a few times she set me up to be in the blogs and get ambushed when we went out to dinner a few times. She's all about herself.

"All right. I'm out for the night, man." We slapped hands and I headed out through the back exit and slid in my car and leaned my head on the back rest closing for my eyes for a second. If Tabitha Griffin was snooping around me again I'd need to let Sutton know to be prepared. She'd probably have us in the papers tomorrow getting married and having a baby.

"Ridiculous," I mumbled to myself, started the car, turned the lights on and pulled off from the back alley way toward home. It was around nine at night, so traffic wasn't as heavy on the main streets.

* * *

THIRTY MINUTES LATER, I pulled into my private parking space in the garage. I eased out of the car and shut the door. I looked up at the security guard and marched through the side door of the private entrance, then went to the elevator doors. They opened, and I stepped on, leaning back in the corner and thinking about the long week I had coming up before the big game.

Less than five minutes later, I made it inside and stripped off my shirt and jacket. I dropped the keys on the hook and went to shower and head to bed. Hopefully, Tabitha had gotten the message and wouldn't bug me again.

ishful thinking would be getting through this interview without having to get out of character. Today, of all days, I'd ended up oversleeping, and then I got a ticket on my car for not moving it on one of the cleanup days. To me, the city was ripping people off with the high costs of street cleaning. Yes, I had a parking space, but I was too tired from work yesterday to even park in my garage. On top of that, I had to deal with Donovan's antics at his parents' house and him taking my phone.

"Asshole," I muttered to myself.

I decided to wear black pants with a white button-up shirt and heels for once since it was a professional setting with photographers around, and possibly TV cameras. What I didn't expect was to spill coffee on myself after picking it up from Cafe Sin. Plus, I had no time to go back home and change, and Sutton had been calling and texting me all morning.

I finally arrived at his condo and waited to be let up to his place. The receptionist was looking at me like I'd stolen something from her.

"What are you doing here again?" the receptionist with fiery red hair and pink lipstick asked.

I needed to remember to stay calm and not let myself be taken out of character. This was the third time she's asked me that question and I politely said what I had to do today.

"Is Sutton on her way down?" I ignored her questions and asked my own.

"I tried calling upstairs but didn't get an answer."

If she didn't wear all that makeup and changed her attitude she would come across as a likeable person.

"There you are!" Sutton called out and I glanced her way and smiled.

"Finally. Waiting forever," I lied. It had only been 10 minutes.

"I tried calling upstairs but didn't get an answer," the receptionist told her.

"Didn't we say to let her up automatically and I left her name with you," Sutton remarked, and my eyes drew into slits.

"Wow." I was speechless after hearing that.

"Sorry, but we run tight security around here," she replied.

"What's your name again?" Sutton asked. She looked at me for help. I kept my mouth closed and headed for the elevator door, then waited for Sutton.

"Lindsey," I heard her say.

"Lindsey, I suggest you do your job and not get on my shit list. I promise it's not a good place to be," Sutton said and sauntered back to the elevator and we got on together when the door buzzed allowing entry.

"Sorry about that," Sutton said.

"No worries, I figured you guys were busy."

"He's still in the shower actually. Early morning prac-tice," Sutton explained, and I nodded.

"Is the photographer here?"

"Yep, and the videographer."

"Do you think the stylist will let me borrow a jacket to cover up?"

I lifted my bag, showing the spilled coffee stain.

"I have my wrap with me you could wear."

The doors opened, and I followed her toward his place. I'd never been to his house, but from Luna's statement, I knew it would be a huge, fancy condo with two floors and high ceilings. Sutton pushed the door open, and my breath caught in a hitch. It was a massive, luxurious, surprisingly open space with photos of his family and football career on the walls. I hadn't expected it to look so cozy and not like a bachelor pad.

I noticed Kaci sitting next to the stylist, looking at the wardrobe. Over in the corner, a photographer was setting up lights. They pushed the glass table back to make space, left the black rug, and put two chairs up—probably for us to sit down and talk.

"Here, you can wear this and do you mind letting the makeup artist touch you up?" Sutton asked.

"Not too much, Sutton. I'm not doing a music video here," I kidded, placed my bag on the couch and sifted through to grab what I needed for the interview.

"I promise." Sutton left me alone to head toward Kaci and I watched her direct everything around me from the food coming out of the kitchen I assume by the chef. They had everything laid out and my stomach started to growl.

"Somebody's hungry," I heard from behind me.

I twisted around, looking at Donovan Hunt's mischie-vous smile. He smelled fresh and clean, with a hint of cologne. He was wearing a black V-neck shirt, black jeans, and socks.

"D, nice to see you again."

The smile dropped from his face. He pressed his chest against me and dropped his hands to the back of the couch, locking me in place.

He leaned close to my ear and whispered, "What did you call me?"

"D... D... your nickname," I stuttered.

He pushed the piece of hair away from my face and our eyes locked in place. I felt a lump in my throat.

"I told you to call me Donovan."

"I like D."

"Really?" He started to reach for his pants and unbuckle, I gasped.

"Are you crazy?" I gritted my teeth and tried to push him away.

"You just said you like D."

"Not like that, asshole," I hissed, smacking his hands from my shoulders.

"Then show me what you like. I aim to please."

"Donny stop messing with her and come over here," Sutton said and I giggled at his expression. Sutton and his mom were the only ones that I know of who would call him Donny to fuck with him as a nickname.

"Sutton, you're blocking true love over here," Donovan said.

"I doubt that," I mumbled and went under his arm and stood to the side of him with my notepad in my hand and tape recorder.

"We'll continue this later, Kam," Donovan said.

I ignored his comment, went to the food table, and picked up a few pieces of fruit to eat while they continued to set up.

"Kamara, you're really close to Donovan right?" Kaci asked.

"Not really, I'm friends with his sister."

"Oh." Kaci looked back at Donovan then toward me.

"So, you aren't sleeping together?"

I nearly choked on the grape I just threw in my mouth and she reached around to pat me on the back. I raised my hand up to let her know I was fine.

"I'm not sleeping with Donovan Hunt!" I screeched loudly, not realizing we weren't alone.

Sutton looked at us curiously.

"Sorry, a blog post just came up on my phone." I pretended my tape recorder was my phone.

"Sorry, it just seemed like you two were very close over there."

"I'm friends with his sister and nothing more."

"Perfect! So, I have a chance with him." Kaci smiled, and twirled a lock of her hair around and went back to helping Sutton.

"We're ready, Kamara," Sutton said.

I picked up a bottle of water and headed over to the makeup artist's chair. I let her place a little foundation on me.

"You really don't need much. Your skin is beautiful," she said, lifting the bronzer and brush.

"Thanks."

"You're all set. It didn't take much."

I stood and checked myself out in the mirror and smiled. The makeup was light and fresh against my skin and gave me a little pop.

"I'm ready, Sutton," Donovan said and I walked over to the middle of the living room and sat across from him and crossed my leg on top of the other, they checked the lighting and backdrop.

"Anytime you're ready, Mara," Sutton said and I nodded, clearing my throat.

"Mr. Hunt, thank you for being here today to talk about the allegations against you."

"Not allegations. They are lies," he replied, staring at me with his hands clasped together in his lap. His legs were wide open, showing off what all the women fell all over themselves about.

"You say lies, Ben and Julian made it seem more like allegations you should be trying to clear up."

He shifted in his seat.

"Tell me this, did you take drugs in college?"

"No."

"So why do you think Julian made that statement?"

"Simple, he's jealous and scared to lose in the big game."

"What about Ben Simmons?"

"He's upset I don't kiss his ass like other people do."

"Do you think your reputation as a lady's man is partially to blame?" I asked, trying to shift the conversation.

"My reputation?"

"Yes. I mean, the women throw themselves at you. Every other day, you're out with another woman."

"I didn't know you paid that much attention to me, Kam," Donovan responded.

My brows shot up in alarm.

"D, it's hard to avoid when it's on every social website. I mean they even have a page for Donovan's girls."

"You sound jealous."

"I'm not."

"Are you sure? I mean, if you feel there's something to explore…" Donovan said, running his tongue over his bottom lip.

I felt warm all of a sudden, hands clammy, throat dry. He was challenging me in front of everyone.

"Let's stay on topic, Mr. Hunt. Are you prepared for the big game?" I asked a simple question to cool the tension.

"I am. Are you going to be there? I know football's not your thing and all. But maybe I could change your mind."

I glanced at Sutton. She was annoyed with the entire thing; I could tell by her posture. She was probably going to hate it after this.

"What do you think your weakness and strength is going into the big day?"

"Can't give away any secrets, sweetheart."

"That means you're holding back."

"It means I let my opponents know I'm ready whenever. Los Angeles Hawks are the team to beat," Donovan bragged.

"Cut!" Sutton yelled and the cameras stopped rolling.

"How'd I do?" Donovan asked.

"D, cut the shit and be professional. We'll probably only have five minutes of this interview that we can use." Sutton rolled her eyes at him.

"I told you I didn't want to do this," Donovan complained as the makeup artist touched him up again.

"I don't care what you don't want to do. Get through this, so I can take a vacation, please," Sutton huffed, throwing her hands in the air and stomping back over to the other side of the camera.

I laughed as Donovan mocked her tantrum.

"Kamara!" Sutton yelled.

I froze.

"Huh?"

"Focus please," Sutton said.

"Sorry," I replied. We went on with more questions and then I watched in the background as he took photos for the Los Angeles Life newspaper and a sports magazine Sutton told me he was getting on the cover of. He was a natural with the camera. I could give him that for sure.

Four hours later I was done and heading home on the freeway and stopped for takeout as my phone rang.

"Hello?" I put my change back in my purse as I juggled the phone and food in my right hand, and purse in my left.

"I was wondering when my child would call her mother."

I chuckled, opened the passenger door, and placed the food down.

"Hi mommy."

"Don't hi mommy me."

"Sorry for not calling you."

"Hmm."

"Stop being grumpy."

"I can be grumpy when my only child hasn't called her mother in forever."

"See, you're getting dramatic; it's only been two weeks."

"Two weeks too long."

"Where's Dad?"

"Don't change the subject."

"I'm not." I started the ignition and checked my mirror before driving off back home on the freeway. The Chinese food smelled good and I couldn't wait to scarf it down while catching up on my reality TV shows.

"Tell me anything. I want you to come for dinner, little lady."

"I will. I promise. This weekend."

"Good, now are you dating?"

"We are not having this conversation."

"Now, you're keeping secrets from your parents."

"Momma, you are getting dramatic again. Stop

watching those soap operas and put down your martinis," I teased.

"I'm not the only dramatic one in this family."

"Who Daddy?"

"No, your cousin Kera. She divorced her second husband and moved back here," Mom explained.

As I drove home, she caught me up on all the juicy gossip about my cousin, who was around the same age as me. We hadn't seen each other in two or three years because she'd gotten married again and moved to Atlanta. Her mom and my mom were sisters, and we were close growing up, but as we got older, she became more interested in money and less in school and her career. I gave up on trying to hang out with her and live her unrealistic dream. Hopefully, she'd come back with a new attitude, and less opinions on my life choices.

Two days later, I let Luna and Sutton talk me into going to a club since it was the weekend, and the interview had aired and made headlines. My social media and newspaper column blew up with notifications, shares, and people wanting me to come on the national circuit and talk about Donovan. I declined for the simple fact that I was a journalist before my interview with Donovan, and I would continue to be one after it. To me, it was a simple interview, but the news media saw more and thought we were dating and keeping it under wraps. I laughed when I read that and blew it off.

Now, I was standing in Club Seduction and wearing the tiniest dress Luna could find and heels that I could barely stand in. I tried to get comfortable as the bottle girl came and brought our drinks.

"I'm loving this music tonight and the men are scrumptious." Luna giggled, sipping on her cocktail. She ordered three *Get Bents* a tequila martini that's supposed to enhance your sex drive. From the looks of the hickey she tried to cover up earlier she didn't need the drink at all. The DJ shouted over the microphone.

"Where are my single ladies at!" the DJ repeated.

"Over here!" Luna stood, pointing at us.

"Luna, sit down." Sutton laughed and pulled her by the arm.

Sutton knew the owner of the club and got us a VIP booth to hang out and chill. I had a drink already and was taking my time with the second one.

"I want to go dance, come on." Luna gulped down the rest of her drink.

"How many of those have you had?" I asked, motioning for the bottle girl that was standing near the rope of our entrance to come here.

"You ladies need something else?" she asked.

"Can you bring us three bottles of water please?"

"Sure thing," she replied, and went back to the bar.

The base of the music strummed through the walls as Nicki Minaj's voice came through. It hyped Luna up and she started popping her little butt in the air. Sutton and I shook our heads and laughed at her. Luna was comical more than anything and I could never get mad at her even when we lived together in college. Sutton slapped her on the ass and stood to dance with her.

"Come on, Kam. You're not working tonight, so get loose," Luna called me out.

I had no choice but to get up and join them on the dance floor. She grabbed my hand and walked us out to the dance floor, and we made our own little area near the DJ booth. I planted my hands on my hips, moved around in a circle, threw one hand in the air, and popped my ass in the air, thanking my momma for giving me my confidence and my shape. I was a nice size, with thick hips, ass, and thighs, and nice, full breasts. But it was tough to find a guy who wanted me for me, and not just my body.

"Get it, Kam!" Sutton screamed, hyping me up. I was glad to have my hair up in a ponytail and not sweating it out from the sweat dripping down my face. Luna came behind me and worked her hips in the same motion and everybody started calling and cheering us on. I changed it up and turned around to dance face to face and grabbed her hands then twirled her around.

"Go, Luna! Go! Go!" I cheered her on as a guy came up behind her. He looked familiar, but I was still tipsy from the drink, so I couldn't make him out.

His hands went around her waist and they looked to be doing more than dancing.

"Really, Sutton!" a loud, masculine voice yelled.

I turned and saw Savion Jennings getting in Sutton and some random guy's face. That only meant one thing, and I was too afraid to move.

"I see the moves you make on the dance floor. I wonder if they match the moves you make in the bedroom." His hot, deep, raspy voice spoke into my ear, and he slid his hands around my waist and jerked me back against his chest.

"D?"

He bit the nape of my neck, then kissed the sting away.

"What's my name?" He trailed kisses near my ear and down to my shoulder as he eased us backwards in the corner out of the view of everyone. I wanted to turn around and curse him out but felt the throbbing in my panties had another idea.

"Three years," I mumbled to myself.

"What's that?" He pushed me gently against the wall and stood in front, pressing his body against mine.

"Huh."

"What's three years?"

I was stuck, again trying to figure out what to say and not let my emotions take over and give in to what I'd been wanting for a while. I lowered my head. "Be strong," I whispered.

He lifted a brow; he probably thought I was crazy. But I had to talk to myself and remember the three years I'd gone strong so far.

"I like you, Kamara."

"What?"

"I've had a crush on you for years. I know you think I'm some playboy, but I'm not doing that anymore."

He looked right into my eyes and seemed sincere, but I didn't know if I could trust him.

"Why me?"

"Why not you?"

I chuckled and tried to push him away.

"Move, Donovan."

"Are you saying you've never thought of me or us?"

"No." I rolled my eyes, avoiding any hint of a lie.

"Kiss me."

"Excuse me?"

"Kiss me. If you don't feel anything then a kiss won't hurt," Donovan challenged.

"I'm not doing-" I was cut off when his lips attacked mine and he gripped my waist and my arms automatically went around his neck and pulled him in close as we moaned through the kiss.

"Mmm." He sucked on my tongue, then slid his hand up my stomach and across my breasts.

I shivered in his arms. He wrapped his arms around my neck and gently pulled me back. I felt weak in the knees and definitely needed to change my panties because they were soaked.

"Go out with me," he asked.

"Okay," I replied, not even thinking of what I just took part in while standing in a nightclub near the bathroom.

"OMG!" I shoved him back.

"What's wrong?"

"I need to get back to Sutton. Savion didn't look so happy with her dancing."

"Savion's not going to hurt her," he said and gripped my wrist.

"We came here together, and I'm not leaving them for anyone. Not even you," I said.

He dropped his head and released my wrist. We both walked back toward the dance floor, but I didn't see either of them, so I decided to head over to the area we had reserved. I didn't see them there, either.

"Where are they?" I thought out loud.

"Follow me," Donovan said and I had no choice since the girls weren't in the place I left them. We went across the walkway and toward the larger VIP area I didn't pay attention to and saw Sutton and Luna sitting with Reuben and Savion, and two other gentlemen I didn't know.

"There you are!" Luna jumped up and ran to me with her arms out.

"You two ditched me."

"Kind of like you ditched us for him," Sutton said and I turned to see Donovan smirking.

"Nothing happened," I said and went to sit next to Sutton.

Donovan stopped me, grabbed me around the waist, and pulled me into the corner, then into his lap.

"Donovan we're in public," I hissed through a whisper and tried to get out of his hold.

"So. Let them see."

"I am not in the mood to fight any of your girlfriends."

"Funny."

"What's with you two?" Luna questioned, hands crossed and head cocked to the side with a wide smile on her face.

"Nothing."

"She asked if I wanted to be her boyfriend," Donovan lied and I smacked him on the arm, and he laughed.

"Luna get your brother."

"I like this visual. Donovan don't hurt my friend, or you'll have to answer to me," Luna demanded and I raised my hands up in exasperation.

"I didn't ask him to be my boyfriend."

"Yet," Donovan said and I glared at him.

He went to kiss me again and I put my hand up to stop him.

"Keep your lips to yourself, playboy."

"I'd love to put them somewhere else though." He winked, and Luna motioned like she was going to gag and we both burst into laughter.

"I'm not fooling with you right now."

"Bro! I'm about to head out and take Sutton home," Savion said.

"Are you sure, Sutton?" Luna asked.

"Luna, you're like a little sister to me, but this is my woman," Savion said, reaching his arm around Sutton's shoulders and pulling her in close.

"Not yet I'm not," Sutton told Savion and kissed his lips.

"I can see a double wedding in the future!" Luna clapped her hands in excitement as Sutton and I rolled our eyes at her. For someone that's sneaking around with her plaything she couldn't talk about anyone having a double wedding.

"I'll see you tomorrow at practice." Donovan and

Savion dapped fists and he walked out with Sutton. I tried to get up again and Donovan tightened his hold.

"Where are you going?" Donovan asked.

"I'm heading out with Luna."

"Sorry boo, I'm not going home. Donovan can take you though," Luna said and my eyes bucked wide in shock.

"We came here together."

"I know, but I had a text message from a friend to meet him." Luna fluttered her long lashes, making me feel guilty for stopping her booty call.

"Fine."

"Great. Call me when you make it in and D. Be nice," Luna said and kissed him on the cheek.

"Looks like it's just me and you, sexy," Donovan said.

"Actually, it's going to be just you, because I'm taking an Uber and going home."

"That's crazy Mara, it's late and I can take you home. Stop being dramatic." His words reminded me of me and my mom. I burst into laughter and he looked at me strange. I waved my hands, wiping the tear that tried to escape down my cheek.

"Sorry, I say the same thing to my mom when she gets going on a rant. She can get dramatic."

"I haven't seen your parents in years. How are they doing?"

"Good." He tapped me on the leg to get up and he stood grasping my hand as he shook up with Reuben and his other two friends as we left the club.

"You're not afraid of the paparazzi seeing us together?"

"No. Why would I be afraid?"

"They're always making it seem like you're married and about to have a child. We're already dealing with one story of lies."

We stepped out of the club, and it was chilly. He removed his jacket and placed it around me, while the valet brought his car toward the front. "I don't mind you being the mother of my child."

I knew that caught her off-guard, but it was the truth if I had my way. Was I ready for kids right then? No, but I knew I wanted someone who was beautiful on the inside and out, who cared about people and had a strong sense of family, plus goals and dreams beyond marrying me.

"Are you hungry?" I asked, turning the heat on in the car to keep us warm.

"What do you have in mind?"

The only place I liked to go to after leaving the club is Mickey's on Third and Fairfax. A small mom and pop diner that's open twenty-four hours. They serve anything from burgers and fries to breakfast food.

"Mickey's on Third. You ever been there?" I turned right at the stop sign letting a couple go through the cross-walk, easing down the street at the light before turning into the parking lot of Mickey's.

"I've gone there a few times." She shifted in her seat and crossed her leg. I placed my hand on her thigh.

"You nervous?"

She leaned against the window and peered over at me.

"Why would I be nervous?"

"Just wondering if the kiss scared you off."

I parked the car, turned it off, removed my seatbelt and turned to my side facing her.

"Nothing scares me." She started to open the door to get out and I stopped her by pressing the lock button.

"When you're with me, you don't open doors."

"Are you an undercover gentleman?"

"Depends upon the situation," I teased, reached over, and lifted her chin and pecked her lips. I opened the door and stepped out and went around the front of the car and opened the door for her and pressed my body against hers and captured her lips again.

"D… mmm," she moaned.

I eased back, releasing her lips.

"Let's go inside." I entwined our palms together, strolled to the door, and held it open for us to enter.

Mickey's son noticed me at once.

"Usual table?" MJ asked and I nodded, leading Mara over to the booth in the corner in the back of the restaurant.

"Kamara nice seeing you again, usually you're with Luna," MJ said, dropping the menus on the table in front of us.

"Hi Mickey, Luna decided to leave me hanging so here I am." I pushed myself back in the booth, eyed Mickey as I watched as her eyes widened in delight to see him. Something about her attention not on me caused a little jealousy.

"Mickey, stop stealing my time with this beautiful lady. You already have a woman," I joked, reaching over and covering her hand with mine. I lifted it to my lips for a kiss.

Kamara shook her head and Mickey grabbed her other hand.

"Beautiful, if this one doesn't do right by you, call me," Mickey said.

"You got it," Kamara responded, and I grunted waving him off as he headed back to the kitchen.

"How often do you come here?" Mara asked.

"Probably too much or I'll order to have the food delivered."

"Do you cook?" she questioned, looking up from the menu.

Cindy came to the table and dropped off glasses of water. She's been married to Mickey for over forty years.

"Mickey told me you were out here," Cindy said, standing with her hand on her hip. She reminded me of my mom with her short stature and brown eyes that seemed to know when I've fucked something.

"Hey Cindy."

"How are you, Donovan? I haven't seen you in a few weeks."

"Good, working and keeping in shape. I had to cut back on the burgers," I said, rubbing my stomach.

"Kamara, what are you doing with this?" Cindy pointed at me.

Kamara giggled while taking a drink of her water avoiding the answer.

"Can we get drinks?" I asked, passing her our menus.

"Sure, give me a few minutes. And Donovan?"

"Yeah."

"You treat her good," Cindy said, walking off.

I put my hands up in surrender.

"Why do I feel like I'm the one that should get the warning to protect my heart?"

"Your reputation is known as the playboy." Kamara crossed her arms and sat back in her seat.

"How many boyfriends have you had?" I questioned, moving away from the conversation of me in the media.

"Not too many, the longest was Lex, a guy I dated for a few months about three years ago."

I choked on my water as she spoke. Kamara picked up the napkin and wiped the table down.

"Wait—you haven't dated in over three years?"

"Something like that. I'm more focused on my career and the guys I've met seemed to be one track minded."

"Are you interested in dating again?" I needed to know if I wasn't alone in feeling this strong pull between us.

"Depends."

"On what?"

"Who the guy is that I'm dating."

Cindy stopped at our table and placed the cheeseburgers and large basket of fries on the table between us. I picked it up and took a bite, wiped my mouth, and watched as she did the same and a small amount of mayo lingered on the side of her lips.

"What if that guy is me?"

"You're not involved with anyone? That's hard to believe."

I dropped the burger and leaned on the table clasping my hands together.

"One thing about me, Kamara, is that I'm honest. Do I have a few girls I've had a causal thing with? Yes. I won't lie. But I want you," I confessed and watched as her expression went from confusion, to surprise, to flattery.

"Luna."

"My sister has nothing to do with who I date," I told her. She looked off to the window, then back at me.

"How about I take you out on an official date?"

"Is that what you do with your casual girls?" she asked.

"No. To be honest, they just want to tell people they slept with me, thinking that's going to get them some type of bragging points."

"I've had a crush on you," she said.

To hear those words fucked with me because I let too long of time pass without making her mine.

"*'Had'?*" My brow lifted in confusion.

"Sometimes you can be an ass, Donovan."

"I want to be your asshole though," I teased and slid out of the booth and came around to the other side and sat next to her with my arm on the back of the booth.

"Okay, I'd like to go out on a date."

"If it makes you feel any better, the time you ran in the bathroom and saw me naked. I wanted you before then." I looked at her and kissed the side of her cheek and she squirmed in her seat.

"You've been blessed in all the ways," Kamara said and I grinned.

The night went on and we continued talking about her ex-boyfriend, Lex. I told her about Tabitha, and how she had recently popped up at the bar. She seemed unfazed. I didn't know whether that was a good thing or not, but I'd do everything in my power to let her know what she meant to me.

Mickey didn't want to charge me, but I left a big tip, as usual, just because of how generous they were to me whenever I came in, and they kept the fans and paparazzi away, so I could have peace like any regular customer.

Eventually, I drove her back home, which took about 30 minutes with light traffic, and I walked her to the door.

I didn't have any intention to take things there so fast, but she surprised me when she let me in her apartment. We'd talked at the diner for hours, and then we came back to her place. The only thing I wanted to do was get her home safe. I knew Luna would be texting and calling nonstop if I didn't make sure her best friend got home.

"Mara, are you sure about this?" I needed confirmation if she really wanted to take such a big step. It would be bad if she declined after thinking it over; I'd need a cold shower to make it through the night.

"Yes, I'm sure." She lifted her sweater dress and removed it, letting it fall on the floor.

I sucked in a breath, looking at the sexiest body I'd ever seen—her perfectly round breasts in her black bra, ready to be devoured with my tongue; her meaty thighs, crying out to held, kissed, and licked. I started to take off my shirt and unbuckle my pants. She stepped toward me to help.

"Kamara, I can't promise to be gentle. I've had a crush

on you for so long, it's taking everything in me to not touch you right now."

"I didn't ask you to be gentle," she replied and dropped to her knees. She smacked my hands away from my belt. She slid her hands into my boxer briefs and stroked my dick.

My head fell back. I was in heaven, and my knees almost buckled, but she held me up with her other hand on my leg. Not wanting to get too far into things, I tapped her on the shoulder to stand, and I lifted her.

She wrapped her legs automatically around my waist and directed me to her bedroom.

"Down the hall on the right." She cupped my face in her hands and sucked on my tongue.

If this was heaven, I never wanted to return to reality. Her sweet smell, soft touch, and warm body had me ready to come in my pants. She surprised me with aggression and biting the side of my neck and pressing a kiss, while grinding her hips.

"Kamara, you keep doing that, and I'm not going to make it." I pushed her bedroom door open and scanned the room. It was how I'd pictured it: white carpet, queen-sized bed, mahogany headboard, matching desk and chair in the corner, where she probably did her writing.

Her hand shifted between us, and she caressed my dick. That took me over the brink, and I dropped her onto the bed, pushing her back and ripping her bra off.

"Donovan!" she screeched and tried to cover herself.

"Fuck that bra." I kicked off my shoes, climbed on the bed, reached over to grip the back of her neck and tongued her down and moved the other hand toward her clit.

"Please... D... oh," she moaned.

Hearing those words was like the breath I needed to keep me moving.

"Mara, you're fucking beautiful, baby." I kissed down her chest, squeezed and tweaked her breasts as I continued fondling her clit.

"Ahhh... yes, Donovan!"

Her hips moved in rhythm with my finger and I bent my head down and licked from the top down to her asshole.

"Ugh! Keep going."

"Mara..." I groaned, feeling her juices drip down my chin.

"OMG! Donovan," she begged, trying to push my head back.

Her body trembled in my arms and drained the last drop, sucking on my fingers. I watched as she came down from her high. Her heavy eyes fluttered low as I slid my hand in my pocket and grabbed a condom out of my wallet and rolled the condom down my dick.

"Hold your legs back."

She looked terrified as I stroked myself.

"I'm asking you again, are you sure about it? We can forget this ever happened."

"I'm sure." She reached over and grabbed my dick, lined him up with her entrance and planted her hands on the back of my ass and pushed me further inside.

"God damn, Kamara... what the fuck?!" I continued in beyond the tip. She was tight and snug. I bent down and licked her one more time, then stuck a finger inside, knowing this was going to be my favorite meal.

"I know. Three years ago was the last time," she muttered.

I pushed back in and rubbed a hand across her stomach as I hit rock bottom. I closed my eyes, and I felt like I was breaking a virgin in. Not wanting to hurt her, I kept my thrusts slow at first to get her comfortable with my size.

"More... ahhh." She thrusted upward, and that sent me over the edge.

I circled my hips, hovering farther over her body and burying my face against her neck. Our moans filled the room, and I growled, feeling the tingling of my orgasm on the brink. Her tiny hand gripped the back of my neck and pulled me in close. She sucked on my ear.

"Ahhh... Mara..." I growled. The heat between her thighs felt like a vise grip around me. I pulled her leg straight up, bent my leg, and moved in and out, watching as our connection intensified. I kissed the back of her ankle, massaging her thighs, while her cries of pleasure overwhelmed her. Her juices covered my dick.

"Oh...Donovan I'm coming," she whimpered, and I drove faster and faster, balls smacking against her ass as I felt her stiffen and release.

"Shit!" I fell on top of her as I came, rolled off, released a breath, and kissed the side of her cheek and rose up to get a towel.

"Where's your bathroom?" I asked.

She could barely keep her eyes open, but she pointed out the door. I chuckled and kissed her on the lips again and went to find it across the hall from her bedroom. I tore off the condom, flushed it down the toilet and washed myself up. I went back to clean her up then tossed the washcloth back on the bathroom counter. I went back in her room and she was under the covers snoring.

"Goodnight beautiful." I kissed the back of her neck and fell asleep behind her in bed.

* * *

THE NEXT MORNING, I didn't feel the warm body against me anymore and I popped my eyes open and saw I was alone in bed. I looked around the room and jumped up to put my pants on to find Kamara. I pulled the door and went to check the bathroom, it was empty. Treaded down the hall and heard low whispers and saw Kamara's eyes widen in shock.

"Where did you go?" I asked, wrapped my arms around her back and kissed her forehead.

"Ahhh! I knew it!" I heard my sister Luna loudly screech. She pushed the door wide open and stepped in, then shut the door and put her hands on her hips.

"Luna what are you doing?"

"I came to have breakfast with my best friend like we always do on a Sunday." She circled the both of us.

"Um. I need to shower really quick. Do you mind?" Kamara asked, gripping my hand.

"Sure, I need to get to the gym and practice anyway. Dinner tonight?" I questioned, placing my hands on her hips and pulling her in close to my chest.

"I'd love that, brother," Luna said.

"Not you."

Luna poked her lip out and sat in the chair.

"Let me spend some time with her, and I'll call you later," Kamara explained.

I forced myself not to take her back to bed and fuck her senseless, causing her to skip out on my sister. I kept thinking about the way she felt in my arms when we fell asleep, and how she curled her leg around mine whenever she turned around in the middle of the night to go for another round, and how she'd ride me, and her sexy moans in my ear that kept me on the cliff's edge.

"Call me soon as you're done, and I'll see where I am, and we can meet up," I said and went to her bedroom and grabbed my shirt and keys, then came back to the living room and saw them sitting on the couch talking to themselves.

"Don't forget call me later." I pressed a kiss on her lips, ruffled my sister's hair, and walked out, hearing her curse me out behind me. I jogged down the steps and went to my car to head home. I needed to shower and get to the gym before practice.

* * *

AN HOUR LATER, my headphones were in my ears, pumping me up while I worked on my cardio on the treadmill. I'd tried calling Savion and Reuben, but neither answered, so I figured they were wrapped up with their women, like I wished I was. I slowed down, pushed the button to lower the levels, and took a drink of water.

"Hey, baby." Tabitha appeared in front of me, wearing bike shorts and a sports bra, with her stomach out and her breasts spilling over the top.

"Tabitha," I said, ignoring her hand on mine.

"You mind helping with me stretches? I could use your expertise," Tabitha said.

"They have a personal assistant you can hire," I replied.

"I don't want them." Tabitha sauntered in close, moving her hand up my arm. I picked it up and moved it away from me.

"We're not on that anymore, Tabitha, relax."

"Your lips say it, but I bet this third leg is wanting to take me up on my offer," Tabitha teased, biting the tip of her finger.

"I can promise he's very satisfied."

"Who are you sleeping with?" she demanded.

I scoffed at her question.

I ignored her question and looked up at the TV screen and saw the latest entertainment and sports news with my name scrolled across talking about the upcoming big game and then a flash of me and Kamara coming out of the club last night, then Mickey's is displayed.

"Fuck!" I muttered and stopped walking and turned the machine off and wiped my face with the towel.

"Who is that girl? When did you start dating her?" Tabitha blasted off back-to-back questions.

"My dating life is mine. I don't owe you answers."

I started to head back and change when Tabitha grasped my arm.

"I thought we could try and make a real thing happen with us this time."

"Tabitha, we both know what we had was just sex. I'm not interested." I looked down at my arm, then back at her. She released me. I went into the locker room and almost bumped into the other person who had fucked up a nice night.

"Hope you're working on your knees; you know your left side goes out quickly," Julian mocked me. He was standing there with a towel around his neck, and two of his teammates chuckled along with him.

"I could wear a blindfold, and still win this game against you," I responded, crossing my arms.

"You're still trying to make yourself relevant," Julian egged on.

"Cheap that you want to say I did drugs, when it was really you."

"That was a long time ago," Julian answered.

"Sure about that? I heard you were at the Mandalay in Vegas going hard. Only difference is I don't talk about my business with other people."

"Julian, I didn't know you were here," Tabitha said from beside me.

Julian looked from Tabitha to me and grinned.

"Tabitha you're looking good, baby." Julian reached

over and gave her a hug.

"You, too. Maybe we could get together," Tabitha said.

"Weren't you just trying to fuck me a few seconds ago?" I announced, and her mouth dropped open in shock.

"No, I wanted to see if we could have dinner like old friends," Tabitha answered.

"Yeah, whatever. If you two don't mind, I have things to do." I walked away, leaving them alone. I went to shower and change my clothes, so I could get to practice. I threw my bag in the backseat and texted Kamara. I strolled to the driver's side, slid the key into the ignition, and drove out of the parking lot.

Me: How's breakfast going?

Mara: Hey. It's going well.

Me: Is my sister hounding you about me?

Mara: She said if you break my heart, she's kicking your ass.

Me: She's not even 5'5".

Mara: Leave my friend alone.

I chortled and decided to call her instead.

"Hello."

"I needed to hear your voice."

"How did it go at the gym?" she asked.

"Fine. I didn't get much in because I was distracted."

"What distracted you?"

"You."

"Me? What did I do?"

"Remembering how you tasted and the way you moaned in my ear."

"Donovan."

"What?"

"I can't talk about this right now."

"Why not?" I taunted, knowing she was out in public.

"You know why."

"I know and I bet you're shifting in your seat from your

pussy getting wet."

She sucked in a breath. "I won't hold you up any longer, but I wanted to let you know before it gets out."

"What is it?"

"They saw us."

"Who saw what?" she questioned.

"I assume paparazzi. It was on one of those gossip shows of me and you leaving the club and restaurant."

"Oh."

"Yeah." I scratched the underside of my chin.

"What are you thinking? Should we-"

"No, I'm not stopping, and I'm not letting you go. You're mine, Kamara, and I'm yours."

That was the last thing I said before hanging up. I prayed that she believed me and trusted me enough to keep our relationship above the madness in our world.

If only I believed it myself.

Two weeks later, I was pushing a shopping cart in the store and picking up my favorite chocolate-pecan ice cream to keep me charged up while I wrote a piece on the City Council situation. Over the past week, I'd researched and found a few mentions of certain local businesses that were being targeted to close down, and one of them was Cafe Sin. I needed to talk with Rodney and Abigail before I wrote it up and got it out to the public.

On top of that, Donovan and I had been dating ever since we came back from the club that night. It had been a little weird talking on the phone and sleeping at each other's place, plus meeting and hanging out with his parents as his girlfriend. When we told them about us, they'd kind of figured everything out already by the way we kept stealing glances at each other. Luna was the biggest giveaway because of her comments about a wedding and a baby coming soon, and I had to hurry up and shut that down because it wasn't in my future at the moment, and we'd never talked about our relationship that way.

"Oh sorry. My mistake." I bumped my cart into a woman as I tried to maneuver around the bread aisle.

"Watch where you're going. Wait I know you from somewhere," she said.

"I doubt that unless you live in this area."

"No, you wouldn't happen to know Donovan Hunt?" she asked, and I felt off about her questioning me about D. Was this a reporter or a woman he's slept with before?

"I'm best friends with his sister," I answered.

"And sleeping with him right? I mean we could probably exchange details of the way he likes to run his hand through your hair when giving him oral sex," she taunted and I jerked back in shock.

"Excuse me."

"Stay away from Donovan. I was there first," she barked, threw the loaf of bread in her cart, and walked off.

I shook my head and finished up at the store and paid for my transaction and gripped the two grocery bags and carried them out of the store to my car when a flash of light blinded me, and I dropped my bags on the ground.

"Kamara Powell, how long have you dated Donovan Hunt?" Another flash of light went off, as I tried to pick up my bags.

"Kamara Powell, is it true you slept with him to get a lead interview?" he questioned.

I stood and pushed him out of the way, ignoring his questions. I yanked my door open and tossed my bags inside. I went to the driver's side, climbed in, and shut the door.

"Miss Powell, we have reason to believe you're not the only woman in his life. Any comment?" the jackass asked and shoved the video camera through my window.

I shoved it back and started my car, then backed up and pulled out of the parking lot. I drove home as fast as I could. I didn't know whether that woman was working with him or not, so I tried to take the side streets to avoid any major lights. I couldn't believe anyone thought I'd gotten a leg up because I was sleeping with someone. I sped down the street and pulled into my parking space, then removed my keys, grabbed my bags, and stomped toward the door. I started fumbling with the key, and the door opened on its own. I'd forgotten that Donovan was already there, taking a nap.

"Let me take those," he said, and I pushed the bags in his hands and rolled my eyes, now regretting saying he could come over for dinner tonight. I yanked off my jacket and tossed it on the couch and put my hands on my face to calm down.

"What's wrong with you?" Donovan called out as he strolled to the kitchen.

"Nothing." I jumped up off the couch and went to my bathroom to wash my face with a cool towel. My energy was all off and I was pissed. The minute I decide to give myself to someone and let things flow, this happened. I splashed the water on my face and stared at myself in the mirror. Donovan knocked on the door, then pushed it open.

"You don't wait for me to say, 'come in'?"

"No why?"

"What if I was using the bathroom?" I crossed my arms.

"I've sucked, kissed, and licked from your toes up to your neck and ear. I've seen it all."

"That's not the point."

"Then what's the point?" he argued and glared at me.

I waved him off and tried to walk out of the bathroom, but he pulled me back inside and planted his hands on my hips.

"Talk to me, Mara."

"I was just ambushed at the grocery store."

"By who?"

"A photographer and some big-chested bimbo with bad highlights questioned me about you. I'm just having a bad day."

His head fell back, and he pinched the bridge of his nose.

"Was she about five-seven with red hair?"

"Yeah. You know her?" I tried to step out of his hold, and he tightened his grip.

"Don't let her get to you. Tabitha's an old friend of mine and I explained to her that I wasn't interested anymore, unfortunately she didn't get the hint," Donovan said and closed the space between us.

"Tabitha, interesting," I said.

He kissed my neck.

"Tell me exactly what she said and the photographer."

"It's not important."

"Yes, it is."

"No. You have a big game coming up, and I don't want you worrying."

"Are you sure?" he asked.

"Positive. I think it'll blow over in no time," I responded and kissed him on the lips.

"I'll get Sutton on it just in case."

"Are you ready to eat?" I said, changing the subject.

"Not food," he groaned, attacking my lips and cupping my ass.

I wrapped my arms around his neck.

"Mmm… let me cook before you distract me."

I stepped around him and went back to the kitchen and put the groceries away as he sat on the couch and watched old tapes of plays.

"Have you spoken to Sutton about Savion lately?" I slid

the grey pot on top of the stove and boiled the potatoes for the mashed potatoes. I set the oven temperature for the baked fish and pinto beans.

"No, should I have?"

"She's not only your publicist, babe. She's also your friend."

"We don't talk about stuff like that."

"I'm surprised."

I turned the heat down, set the food on the stove, and let it sit, then went to sit next to him on the couch.

"Enough about everyone else. How are you doing at the newspaper?"

"So far, the response from the interview went well, but as you know, someone thought it was interesting that we started dating right after the article was published."

"I didn't date you because of the article or use you if that's your worry." Donovan lifted me onto his lap, and I straddled him.

"I know, but it's hard to make it in this business as a woman, let alone a woman of color."

He rubbed his hand up and down my back.

"You want me to go around kicking people's ass that fuck with you? I will, you know."

I giggled at his protective nature and kissed his cheek.

"I think you have enough press coverage without fighting my battles."

"I don't care. I'll do it for you." He tilted his head and bit my breast.

I smacked him on the arm.

"Focus," I said.

He shook his head no and tweaked my nipple.

"Thank you for offering," I gasped, grinding my hips on his lap.

"What story are you working on right now?"

"A story about the local City Council, trying to buy up businesses." He slid his hands under my shirt, squeezing my breasts.

"Take this off," he demanded, and I lifted my shirt.

"We didn't go the traditional route of dating for a while, and I never asked you to be my girl."

"No, we didn't."

He stood and I wrapped my legs around his waist.

"Ahhh! What are you doing?"

He placed me on my back on the couch.

"I told you I'm hungry."

"Baby the food."

"Ugh. Fine we eat first and then you get naked on the bed face down, ass up." He slapped my thigh gently and pecked my lips. I jumped up, tried to grab my shirt to put it back on and he yanked it back.

"No shirt."

"You want me to cook without a shirt on?"

He licked his lips.

"Yep. Take your pants off, too."

I cackled at him.

"I'm not taking my pants off. Finish working or something."

"You've distracted me and now I can't work anymore," Donovan joked, wiggling his brows and rubbing his hands together.

"That's a lie. You pulled my shirt off." I walked into the kitchen, and he followed me.

"I don't recall that," he teased.

I smacked him with a towel, and he came up behind me and wrapped his hands around my waist. He kissed the side of my neck as I continued to cook dinner. We ended up getting so full after dinner that we lay on the couch and watched a movie, then fell asleep.

At some point, he must have carried me to bed because I woke up with him in bed in the middle of the night, with his leg across my thigh. I felt a sudden shift in the bed, and my breath hitched from his soft lips on my neck. His body hovered over me.

"What are you doing to me?" I whimpered, reaching my hand out to rub the side of his face as he kissed alongside my shoulder.

"Making you mine," Donovan said and I felt the tip of his shaft poking my ass.

"Mmm... ahh... shit."

"Baby...fuck this is unreal," Donovan said, and started stroking slowly.

"Oh...I'm going to be late for work," I tried to claim.

"Ugh...I'll write you a note," Donovan said and I giggled. He circled his hips, grabbed me by the waist and pumped faster.

"Ahhh. Keep going."

"Mara... ahhh... shit."

Donovan and I orgasmed at the same time. We fell back to sleep with him still inside me.

KAMARA

I practically had to promise Donovan that I would give him a blow job later that night, so I could get out of bed and get to work on time. Before I headed to work, I wanted to stop and talk with Terry and Rodney about the City Council situation. I parked my car and looked around to see if I could find Terry. He wasn't out front like he normally was on a Tuesday morning. I got out of the car, shut the door, and walked toward the alleyway to see if he was sleeping in his normal spot. I didn't see him, so I decided to grab a coffee and talk with Rodney.

"Kam, are you getting your usual?" Abigail asked. I smiled seeing she was working at this location today.

I stepped up to the front of the counter and nodded.

"Where have you been? Rodney's been holding down this location by himself and my drinks don't come out the right way," I whispered with my hand on the right side of my mouth, going into my purse to grab money.

"I know, girl. I had to cover for a few days while the

manager was out sick." She picked up a hot cup and made my drink.

"I heard some things about the businesses around here."

"What do you mean?"

"Terry said the City Council was trying to sell the buildings and create a mall."

She had a sad and disappointed look on her face and glanced around the shop. It was mostly me and one other person sitting in the back corner typing on a computer.

"Terry's right, we got a letter in the mail about them possibly building a new mall," Abigail explained.

"Can you fight this? I mean you pay on time. We have enough big businesses around."

"I feel the same way, but you know unless people rally together nothing gets done," Abigail said.

"Maybe my article will help get the word out."

"Maybe, but I hear you're dating the big star now. So, what's the truth? I saw on social media you two holding hands in the mall," Abigail said as she filled the cup with almond milk and steamed it.

"Not for a lack of trying to keep my private life private, but photographers have been hounding me."

"Did you tell D?" Abigail asked.

"Not really. I just want my life to be simple like it's always been."

"Too late for that, babe. Just remember to keep people out of your business and don't trust the blogs or anyone that says they know Donovan besides his family."

"Some girl the other night tried to tell me to stay away from him."

"You're kidding?" Abigail said, pouring the milk in my cup with whipped cream on top and chocolate sauce.

"Serious as a heart attack. I was at the grocery store."

"I told Donovan about these bimbos coming up everywhere," Abigail explained.

"I usually ignore the groupies but keep me updated about the shop."

I left a five-dollar tip in the jar and headed out of the shop and saw Terry sitting on the bus bench. I walked over to him and sat.

"Pretty lady, I haven't seen you in forever," Terry said, eating a bagel.

"When's the last time you've eaten real food?" I questioned. He shrugged.

"You know there are shelters to help."

"I'm fine. What are you drinking?" he questioned, and I slid in my purse and grabbed five dollars to give him something to drink.

"Get something to drink and eat. I wanted to know if you heard anything else about the businesses around here."

"Only that a vote is coming up soon."

"Mmm."

"You can't be superwoman for everyone, pretty lady."

"I know, but it doesn't hurt to let my voice be heard."

"How's that rich football player boyfriend doing?"

"He's fine."

"Good, long as he treats you right."

"Kamara Powell?" I heard behind my back and turned to look over my shoulder at a photographer holding a camera.

"Don't you guys have a life?" I fussed, standing and crossing my arms.

He reached in his pocket and pulled out a business card. "Our life is following the story. I'd love to get an exclusive of you and Donovan. Maybe a dinner date?" he asked.

I took the business card and scanned the name: *Ben Simmons Productions*.

I pushed it back toward him.

"No thank you." I went toward my car as he continued following me.

"We can make this easy or hard. Just a matter of time before he has another woman on his arm," the guy said.

I opened my car door.

"Then when that happens, you'll have a story. Until then, I'm not discussing my life with you or anyone else," I said and got in my car, put the key in the ignition and pulled out ignoring him taking pictures of the back of my car.

* * *

Twenty minutes later, I was sitting in my office, reading the details on the upcoming City Council vote, when my editor came knocking at my door.

"What do you have for me, Kamara? My assistant said you wanted to talk with me as soon as I came in today." I stood and walked toward my office door and shut it.

"The City Council."

"Okay, what happened?" She sat back in the chair and waited for a response.

"You said if I do the Donovan Hunt interview, I would be able to pitch and get any story I wanted."

"With some restrictions of course."

"I have a source that says the City Council is planning to push businesses out of the area on Griffin and 4th Avenue to open a mall."

"What proof do they have?"

"Mostly hearsay."

"You know how I feel about that."

"I understand, but this story could be big for the paper."

"I need more than a possible gut feeling, Kamara."

I sat at my desk, typed in the upcoming calendar of events for the local city and saw they have a vote pending. I turned my computer to my editor to check it out.

"So, they have a vote coming up. It doesn't mean anything," Cailey said.

"Unless they try to push it through without anyone noticing. I have a friend that owns a business in the area."

"So, this is about trying to save your friend's business? Kamara you have to be impartial in this business."

"I agree and ninety percent of the time I am, but this hits close to home."

"Does this have anything to do with your relationship being public now and using your title as Donovan's girl-friend to get noticed?" she asked.

"No, I would never even think to do that. He's too wrapped up in the game; I haven't had a talk with him about my work."

"I think this is a wild goose chase."

"You hired me to write what I want on an issue I feel passionate about. I won't stop now just because I did a quick celebrity interview."

"It would never cross my mind to hold you back, Kamara. Just be careful about running after empty stories." She stood and left my office.

Was I running after a story that didn't exist? Or was I using Donovan to get ahead? That was my new normal: being aware of him in my life and taking every precaution not to cross the lines.

A knock came at my door, and I looked up, seeing Luna step inside and take a seat on the couch.

"I'm hungover," Luna blurted out.

"Another night with your play toy."

"Something like that. Are you going to your parents' house tonight?"

"Yeah, they asked me to come over and I know Donovan is training for the game."

"Did you get your pass for the game?" Luna questioned.

"Not yet, but Donovan said he'll take care of it."

"Let me know if he forgets, my brother's an idiot some-times, but I love him."

"Did he ever talk to you about a girl named Tabitha?"

"Please tell me she's not back?"

"So, you know her?" I inquired.

"She's a straight-up gold-digger who wants my brother only for his money, and what he can do for her," Luna said.

"I met her at the grocery store the other night."

"Just be careful. She's quick to start something and run."

"Too late for that."

"What do you mean?"

"I can't say if they're working together, but a photogra-pher showed up right after she left."

"Tell my brother."

"It's not a big deal right now."

"Doesn't matter Kam, she'll try and squirm her way back into his life."

"I'll keep that in mind."

"Good, let me go and try to do some work. Are we having dinner at your place with Sutton this weekend or not?" Luna asked.

"Let me get back to you. I have a deadline and Donovan has the game coming up, plus my parents want me to come over more. Everybody decided to demand my time," I stated, shaking my head.

"Remember I come first after the parents, boyfriends come and go, but besties are forever." Luna held her pinky finger out and I locked mine in with her and shook on it.

"Thanks for reminding me."

Luna left my office, and I researched more on the

proposal for the mall. I found that nothing had been sent out to residents about the upcoming vote, or any information about whether it would even be on a ballot for a vote. I stayed in my office for the next few hours, typing up a report that stated my point of view and sending it off to Cailey for print. If it was true, then every business owner should have been made aware of it, along with residents who loved the local businesses and shops that they frequented.

I felt my phone vibrate and took it out of my pocket. I saw that Donovan was texting me.

Big D: You owe me.

Me: What do I owe you?

Big D: Sex.

Me: You told me sex before a game isn't good.

Big D: We still have two weeks to go.

Me: LOL! I was trying to prepare you.

Big D: Baby, there's not enough preparation in the world to keep me from what's between your thighs.

Me: Fine. After I have dinner with my parents.

Big D: Good.

Me: Hey, really quick, I had another photographer stop me.

Big D: About what?

Me: It's not a big deal, but they asked me about an exclusive interview.

Big D: Did they leave a name?

Me: Ben Simmons Productions.

Big D: I figured. He has it out for me. Just ignore him.

Me: I will. Let me get back to work. See you tonight.

* * *

THE DAY WAS LONG, but I had to make a stop at my parents' house for dinner and what I found was a complete surprise when I showed up and saw Donovan here already talking with my parents.

"Hey, Mara, baby," Dad said and hugged me.

I dropped my purse on the couch.

"Hi Dad, what's going on here?" I pointed at Donovan.

"He surprised us with a visit," Mom said and took the bottle of wine I brought to the kitchen.

Donovan walked toward me and kissed me on the cheek.

"I thought you had a late practice," I said.

"Coach gave us a break," Donovan said.

"So, Donovan, tell me. What are your intentions with my daughter?" Dad said and I groaned, dropping my face in my hand. Donovan laughed, lifted my hand, and kissed the back of it.

"Sir, I plan on making her very happy—the same way she makes me happy," Donovan said.

"Good, because the last guy, Lex or something, was an asshole. Kamara could have done so much better," Dad argued and I rubbed the tension from my neck.

"Dad, can we keep my love life out of this?"

"He needs to know in case he gets out of pocket and I have to have a talk with him." Dad's army ways came out sometimes when he was passionate about something.

"I understand, sir, but my job is to keep her happy," Donovan said, pushing a piece of hair behind my neck.

"How are you feeling about the upcoming game?" Dad said.

"I think I will bring another win home," Donovan informed me as my mom came into the living room.

"Time for dinner," Mom said.

We all stood and walked into the dining room.

"This looks good, mom," I said and sat next to my Dad and across from Donovan.

"All of your favorites," Mom replied.

"How is work going, Mara?" Dad questioned.

I picked over the smoked mozzarella pasta and salad.

"I might have a big story coming up, it just depends."

"On what?" Dad said.

"If my editor likes the direction I'm going."

"What's it about?" Mom asked.

I wiped my mouth of the sauce and ate another piece of garlic bread.

"It has to do with the City Council having a vote on local businesses on Griffin and 4th."

"Isn't that where Rodney and Abigail have Cafe Sin?" Donovan questioned and I nodded.

"Yeah, and my editor thinks it's a lost-cause type of story, or I'm using my status as your girlfriend to push it through—even though I told her I wasn't doing that," I explained.

"You would never use anyone to get ahead. Maybe your editor needs to talk with me," Mom announced.

I chuckled. Ever since I was little, she thought she could fight all my battles for me.

"You're the last person I would think would be using me. Hard enough to get you to go out with me in public," Donovan teased.

"Ouch." I kicked his leg under the table.

"Kamara leave him alone. You were the same way with Lexington," Mom complained.

"Please don't bring up Lex." I waved my hand.

"Donovan is it possible to get tickets for the game?" Dad asked and embarrassment was written all over my face.

"Dad really?" I commented.

"Sure, I can get you tickets," Donovan replied.

"You don't have to do that, Donovan," I said.

"I want to," Donovan responded.

"I knew he would be a good fit for you, Kamara," Dad said.

I filled my mouth with more pasta, trying to avoid the awkwardness.

"I've been telling her that, sir," Donovan joked.

I kicked his leg under the table again.

*D*inner with her parents went great, and I was feeling pumped after practice earlier, so I needed to be buried deep in her pussy to get a good night's sleep. This past week had been nonstop, waking up in the early morning and getting a workout in before heading to practice and learning plays, then interviews back-to-back, and I hardly had time to spend with my baby.

I kicked the door closed and ripped her shirt open, then sucked on her tits as her mouth hung open in ecstasy. We fought to get my pants down. I kicked off my shoes, and she did the same, and then took off her pants. She turned with her back to my chest. I cupped her breasts with one hand and ran my other hand down her stomach to play with her clit.

"Let's go to bed," she mumbled, reaching her hand out to grab the back of my neck and kiss me on the lips.

"You on top," I muttered and smacked her on the ass and watched her walk in front of me swishing her hips.

She turned around and motioned me to follow her with her finger toward the bedroom. She opened the door and pointed toward her bed, and I kissed her on the lips again, making sure to leave her wanting more.

"I missed you, too," she said.

The last time we were together really was after her parents' dinner. After that I was either too busy or she was slammed with work at the office. On top of that the news reports kept saying I was too wrapped up in women to have time for a girlfriend, and I wanted to ask Kamara if she had seen the articles.

"Fuck!" I groaned, as she gripped my shaft, licked the tip, and sat up and eased down slowly.

"Tell me what you're thinking."

"I'm thinking about how I can lock us away in here forever," I muttered, pushed up off the bed, and wrapped my arms around her waist. She grinded back and forth with her arms around my neck as I sat up and kissed her on the lips. The feeling of vulnerability when she's in control does something to me and drives me insane with want and need.

"Baby!" I cried out, not caring how it made me sound.

"I know. Keep going," she moaned, pushing me back to lie flat. She turned to the reverse cowgirl position and kept her feet at an angle with her hands on my thighs. I watched as she slid up and down on my girth. Her skin glowed as sweat filtered down her body and onto the sheets. I clutched her hips and pushed a finger in her butt. My pace became faster, and I gripped her hair in my hand and pumped in and out. Soon, her walls tightened around me and her moans and panting got louder.

"Donovan please!"

My eyes start to feel blurry and my balls draw up ready to release.

"Oh Fuck! Kamara." I ran a hand across her back and ass, and she turned around facing me while still on top.

"Oh... I'm almost there," she said, licking the side of my neck.

I wrapped a hand gently around her throat and stared into her eyes.

"Come for me," I said and the look in her eyes was the most beautiful thing I had ever seen and right after, her release covered the bed sheets. I moved her next to me as we were both spent and trying to control our breathing back to a steady rate.

"That was amazing," Kamara said.

I lifted her chin and kissed her again, running a hand down her arm.

"I want you sitting in the box seats for the game next week."

She screwed her face in a frown.

"What about your parents and sister?"

"They'll be there too."

"Are you sure? You probably have friends that want to get a front row seat."

"I'm positive and invite your parents too."

"Okay."

"Good."

"Hey, I wanted to talk to you about something," she said.

"What is it?"

"I didn't go into too much detail, but the Ben Simmons guy tried calling me about the interview."

I moved back and sat up against the headboard.

"What did he say?"

"I guess the reporter guy that passed me his card that one time I was talking with Terry told him to contact me, but I was avoiding his calls."

"Shit." I ran a hand across my face.

"Should I be worried?"

"Ben's all about ratings, and if he can fuck my life over, then he will. By any means."

"Why not do an interview with him?"

"Because he wants to show off like he's some hotshot reporter, but mostly deals with gossip and lies."

"Is that what happened with Julian?"

"Julian's the one that dealt with drugs in college and I found him passed out one night from an overdose and called for help. He tried to play it off and he almost lost his scholarship, but I put in a good word for him."

"But he still holds a grudge?"

"Possibly has something to do with the women always wanting me over him." I shrugged and she rolled her eyes and tried to get out of bed.

"Where are you going?"

"Away from you. I need to shower and head home."

"I want you to stay here for the night. It's late anyway."

She yawned. I rubbed her thigh, leading up to her breast.

"Going to sleep, Donovan, you should too."

"One round and I'll go to sleep."

"I have work in the morning, your one round turns into all night."

"I promise, baby. Mmm-hmm... one more round." I pecked her lips and pushed her back onto the bed. She opened her legs, and I eased back inside her core.

* * *

THE TIME KAMARA and I had spent together was more than fulfilling and satisfying—and that was beyond just the sex. She was everything I'd hoped for and needed in my life, and one day, I hoped to see little Kamaras running around.

At the moment, though, sitting inside Sutton's office, I

felt like pulling my hair out and like I might end up in jail because of the way Kaci was throwing herself at me. Sutton was running late from a meeting, and she'd arranged for me to come in to go over some commercial opportunities that she'd lined up. Kaci had other plans, and I wasn't in the best mood after what Kamara told me about a photographer approaching her to do an exclusive shoot.

"Come on Donovan, no one has to know."

Kaci rubbed her hand across my chest.

"How much longer is Sutton going to be?" I asked.

Kaci shrugged and unbuttoned the top of her jacket and I scratched the back of my neck and released a harsh breath.

"Kaci we've been through this. I have a girlfriend."

"Nothing wrong with having someone on the side for when you get bored with her." Kaci ran a hand down toward my dick and squeezed.

I pushed her away.

"What the fuck, Kaci?"

"You know most guys would be flattered," Kaci shouted.

"What is going on in here?" Margaret rushed into the office.

We both turned around.

"Nothing Margaret. I was just helping Donovan figure out something on his schedule," Kaci mentioned and I narrowed my brows.

"You mean Mr. Hunt," Margaret said.

"Huh?" Kaci replied.

"Call him Mr. Hunt, not Donovan," Margaret responded.

"That's what I meant," Kaci said.

"I'm sure it was but please keep this door open at all times. I know Sutton wouldn't want anything inappropriate happening in her office," Margaret commented.

I mouthed, *thank you for saving me.* Kaci's underhanded flirtations were getting out of hand, and I hated to bring it to Sutton's attention because often, I could handle it on my own. But now that I was with Kamara, I didn't want anything getting back to her that would put me in a bad light.

"I'm so sorry I'm late." Sutton waltzed inside and I continued to stand in front of her desk.

"Take a seat D, we have a few things to cover," Sutton explained and I shook my head.

"I'm fine with standing."

"Okay, is everything all right." Sutton looked between me, Kaci, and Margaret.

I glanced at Kaci to see if she would tell the truth.

"What's going on?" Sutton said.

"You want to tell her?" I asked.

"I... I have some calls to make," Kaci said and walked out of Sutton's office.

"What was that about?" Sutton asked me.

"Nothing. Can you tell me what the big news is that made you want me to stop practicing and come here first?"

She sat at her desk and clasped her hands.

"Paolo got you an endorsement with Millennium sports gear."

"Yeah so."

"Well, they want me to handle the publicity roll out and Paolo asked me to handle the commercial concept with social media." Sutton cheered and clapped her hands.

"Good job, I guess," I said.

"Donovan, you're such an asshole." Sutton laughed at me.

"You know I am happy for you Sutton, but you could have called me about this."

"Maybe, but I saw the latest Tabitha and Julian posts

and wanted to get your thoughts." Sutton held up her phone and showed me the social media accounts.

@QueenTabitha: Donovan's lying in my bed. He's not claiming that bitch Kamara.

@JulianA: Once we win, you'll see the real MVP in this game.

"More of this posted, so I wanted to know how you want me to handle this," Sutton asked.

"Put out a statement that it's lies on both statements," I responded.

"What does Kamara think of everything?"

"We haven't really talked that long about it, honestly."

"Please don't have my friend out here looking stupid, Donovan," Sutton told me.

"That's not me, Sutton. Have I played around in the past? Yes. But Kamara is different."

"Then you need to put something out to put a stop to the lies."

"I trust you to handle it for me," I said and kissed the side of her cheek and stepped out of her office and saw Margaret sitting back at her desk.

"Go ahead, say it."

"You don't need my opinion in your head," Margaret said.

"I don't, but I respect your opinion."

"Well, you're young and want to think things will just disappear, but you're in the big leagues and you know better than anyone. If they can twist the truth to fit what they need, they will," Margaret explained and I nodded.

"You're right."

"I like Kamara for you. So, treat her right and make sure you win the game and show Julian who's the real MVP."

"Are you coming with Sutton?" I questioned.

"No, we need someone at the office to stay on top of things, but I can watch from her office," Margaret said.

I leaned over and kissed her on the forehead, and she smiled.

"Until next time, Margaret."

"Until next time, Donovan."

Afternoon traffic was insane on the road to the stadium in Inglewood. I didn't want the coach to start yelling at me about being late, so I told Savion to tell him that I was picking up my mother from the doctor. I knew it was a lame excuse, but anything to keep the coach off my ass.

I jogged into the stadium and saw Julian standing at the entrance and talking to some guy.

"Well look what the cat dragged in," Julian said.

"I see you're buying what you need to get your performance up," I joked.

"Actually, he's a reporter asking questions of how we're going to kick your ass in the game."

"Mr. Hunt, is there any truth to Kamara Powell trying to investigate the City Council's voting block being held up?" he asked.

I remembered Kamara saying something about her job but didn't remember all the details.

"No comment."

"She's on the record saying that representatives are pushing local businesses out by building a mall and raising taxes," he informed me.

"Kamara the girl you've been seen around town with right? She's sexy, I wonder how she'd feel around my dick," Julian joked and the reporter laughed. I punched him in the face, not even thinking of the consequences.

"Leave my girl's name out of your mouth."

"You're just pissed I've had Tabitha, and I'll have Kamara real soon," Julian taunted.

I went to punch him again, but the security guard pushed me back.

"Mr. Hunt, is this what you do? Go around punching people in your girlfriend's honor? I mean, your name is spread around the tabloids as dating Tabitha, and some other woman—I think she's named Kaci," he said.

I jerked back in shock.

"What did you say?" I was in disbelief.

"I have a source that said you're dating a woman name Kaci," he said.

"Who's your source?" I asked.

"I can't give that away," the reporter said.

"Yeah, because it's a bogus story, from a bogus source. Get the fuck out of here." I pushed him away and marched into the stadium and went to work out and prepare for the game and get my mind off the bullshit of people trying to piss me off.

An hour later, I was circling the gym and drinking water, trying to relax my mind, when Reuben approached me with my phone.

"Bro, your phone is blowing up." Reuben handed it off to me.

Kamara: Did you see this?

She linked me to an article called "Love in Sports", and I skimmed it: *"I don't talk about my private life, and what Donovan and I have is personal,"* Kaci was quoted as saying.

Me: You can't believe that shit.

Kamara: Why is she talking like you have something going on?

Me: I turned her down, and she's pissed. That's all.

Kamara: Donovan, you need to get a handle on all this mess.

Me: I can't control the media, Mara.

Kamara: You should be able to control who you sleep with.

Instead of continuing the back-and-forth text thing I decided to call her.

"Why are you letting this bullshit get in your head?" I questioned.

"I'm just tired of the nonstop emails, calls, and notifications from women, blasting how good you are in bed and asking what you see in me."

"Baby fuck them. You're who I go home too and wake up next to. That's all that matters."

"Just get this handled please."

"I'll try. But the story with the City is that straightened out?"

"Why do you ask?"

"I got confronted by a reporter about the story."

"So, they're going to you to force me to stop doing my work now," Mara yelled.

"Calm down, Mara. It's not like that."

"You can say that. But I'm still building my career." She sighed and released a breath.

"What's that supposed to mean?"

"It means I need to get back to work," she said and hung up before I could reply.

I grunted and tossed the phone on the ground in frustration, then went back to working out.

Sunday was approaching fast. The crowd surrounded us as the sun went down. This was my second time making it to the big game after seven years in the league. We'd come close with winning division championships but getting to this level after so many years was a blessing. I didn't know if I had anything left in me as a quarterback, but the outpouring of support from fans showed they still believed in our team.

The coin toss went up, and the kickoff started, with Julian's team bringing it down the field. I looked up at the stadium, watching as my family and Mara clapped their hands when we intercepted the ball and had a chance to score our first touchdown.

"Let's Go Hawks!" Savion shouted, pumping everyone up.

"Donovan, it's up to you. Hold the line, focus on the end zone," Captain explained, pointing at the clipboard of one of his plays we've run through at practice.

"1, 2, 3, Hawks!" we all screamed and got back on the field.

I held the ball in my hands, gripping it firmly, feeling the lining and the rubber logo. I positioned myself behind Reuben, glanced both ways, closed my eyes, and breathed.

"Hut 1! Hut 2! Pop left!" I shouted, running the play as everyone scattered. I checked who was open but before I could get the ball out of my hands, I was hit from the side and went down on the field.

"Fuck!" I dropped the ball.

"Boo! Boo!" The crowd got antsy. The referees came on the field.

"Come on. You got this," Savion said, slapping hands with me.

I glanced over at Kamara in the stands. She smiled and waved as I moved back into position to run the play again. Since the phone call at the gym that day, we'd been spending time together off and on. Her focus had been on the shit that was going down with Rodney and Abigail's store, and I'd been slammed with practice and preparing for today.

* * *

THE HALFTIME SHOW STARTED, while we sat in the locker room, trying to figure out where we went wrong. The coach basically rammed it down my throat that I was distracted and not focused. Then Savion got hurt and was getting his ankle looked at. I took a gulp of water and poured some over my head to cool off.

"We need to get back on track. This is not the team I know," Coach said.

"Coach, we know the reason we're losing," Walter, the offensive running back, said.

"What's that supposed to mean?" Reuben spat, standing up.

"Your boy can't handle the pressure," Walter shouted and jumped up.

"Say it to my face," I argued and got up to defend myself.

"Hey! That's enough!" Coach shouted, pushing Walter to sit back down.

"Coach we all see it. He's getting the big bucks, but he's a joke," Walter responded and I dropped my water bottle and charged toward him, but Reuben and few other teammates got in between us before I could punch him.

"Wait til the game is over," I challenged.

"Come at me now! Think you're all that." Walter's nostrils flared as he pushed Reuben's hand off of his shoulder.

"Shut this down now! Get this aggression out on the field," Coach demanded, and we all stopped.

"We're down by ten points. We need to play as a team." Savion came back in the room on crutches.

"Tell that to your boy," Walter sarcastically commented. He was standing against the locker door with his arms crossed.

"Walter, one more comment and you're out," Coach said and ran a hand down his face.

"Five minutes!" the security said, before we had to get back out on the field for the second half. A variety of singers put on a halftime show from rock, pop, and R&B. No matter what happens I know this will be talked about for a while, how I dropped the ball and led us into the big game without a clear plan of execution.

A few seconds later, we piled back onto the field, and everything went in slow motion as our rivals stopped every ball I threw. A few times, I got tackled. The score was 20 to 21, with New York in the lead. We were going for an onside kick to recover the ball and try for a field goal to take the win. The whistle blew, and I watched as New York recovered the onside kick, taking possession of the ball and running time off the clock, winning the game. After months of work and grinding, we all watched as it flew over our heads, and the entire field was covered in their fans and friends. I dropped my head in frustration and walked off, not wanting to talk to any reporters, but luck was not on my side for the second time that night.

"Donovan! Donovan! How do you feel about your performance?" Ben Simmons said.

"No comment." I tried to walk around to the locker room.

"Do you think you could have been distracted by your love life?" Ben shoved the microphone in my face. I jerked back at his question. Having my personal life on national TV was rude and caused me to blow up. Lately I've seen a few posts talking about me and Kamara's relationship.

"What did you say?"

"I said, 'your little girlfriend'. Is she a distraction? Or maybe you and Tabitha are back together? Which one is it?" Simmons smirked.

I didn't know what came over me because the next thing I knew, I was sitting in the locker room with Coach, who was yelling at me for punching Ben in the nose. I opened and closed my hand, feeling the throbbing pain from hitting him as the team doctor put an ice pack on my hand.

"What were you thinking?" Coach asked.

I blew out a breath, trying to figure out how to explain what I did.

"Coach you don't understand."

"You're right. I don't."

"He was talking shit about my girl."

"What are you three years old!" he shouted as he threw my helmet across the room.

"Whatever."

"Son, I'm going to pretend you didn't just disrespect me like that. I understand that your head's all screwed-up after losing the game. Take some time to get your head straight," Coach preached.

I nodded, went to my locker, and grabbed my things to leave. Savion and Reuben came to pick up their gym bags and followed me as security escorted us through the hall. I wasn't in the mood to play nice and give fake interviews and say we played our best, or any of that type of shit. That would only give Julian more ammunition to gloat and cause me even bigger problems.

The door opened at the front entrance of the private section for players, and I saw my family and Kamara's parents next to her. The expression on her face was concerned, and I didn't really feel up to being bothered with anyone.

"Son, you did your best. You'll make it next time," Dad said. He reached out to put his hands on my shoulders and hug me.

"Thanks Dad, but I'm not really in the mood to talk with everybody now. You mind if I skip out on dinner?" I asked.

He nodded, glancing at my mom.

"You know she's going to call you first thing in the morning to see how you're feeling. Don't shut us out," he said.

"I know, let me talk to Kamara really quickly."

"Sure," Dad said.

Kamara walked over and stood on her toes to give me a kiss.

"I'm sorry about the game," she said.

"Yeah, I know."

"Are you going to your parents? I can follow you," Kamara said.

"I need some alone time if you don't mind."

"Away from me?" she asked.

"I just need to get my mind right, it's a lot happening and I'm fucked up about the game."

"I understand, but it might be good to talk it out." She ran her hand up my chin and stared in my eyes.

"I'll call you." I pressed a kiss on her lips and walked off to Savion's car and waited for him to open the door while he talked with Sutton. I avoided my sister's glare and Kamara as I scrolled through my phone. A few minutes later Savion unlocked the door of his Jeep and we got in and he drove off.

"You know that was fucked up right?" Savion said, driving with one hand on the wheel.

"What are you talking about?"

I looked at the missed text messages from women saying how they can make me feel better and that I should break up with my girlfriend and focus on the game more. One DM popped up from Kaci of her naked and pleasing herself while she watched the championship game.

"Kamara and that bullshit excuse of you needing space."

"Yeah, I agree with Savion and you know I don't do relationships. But that was a low blow brother," Reuben started from the backseat.

"She'll be fine." I closed my messages. Tabitha's name came up with a voice message alert.

"I know your head is all screwed up, but we'll get them next time," Savion told me.

I bit the inside of my cheek. I couldn't believe I'd fumbled so much in a game against Julian, and it had been on national TV for the world to see.

"He's never going to let me live this down." I banged my hand against the door.

"D, you break my window you're paying for a new car," Savion said.

"Plus, paying for my emotional abuse."

"What the fuck do your emotions have to do with his window?" I turned in my seat and looked at him.

"I mean you acting up might cause me to not get laid tonight," Reuben muttered, and I flipped him off.

"Bro don't make me kick your ass. You and my sister aren't hiding anything if that's what you're trying to do. Everyone knows about you two."

"I wasn't hiding, your sister wanted to keep us low key," Reuben complained.

Savion pulled up to my place forty minutes later and I slapped hands with him and Reuben and stepped out, strolled through the main entrance and walked by the receptionist desk.

"Sorry about the game tonight, Mr. Hunt," the receptionist said.

"Thanks." I kept my head down, not paying her any mind.

"If you need some company let me know. I'm off in ten minutes," she flirted.

I hit the button to my floor and jumped when the door opened.

"Not in the mood for company."

She leaned over the desk as the doors closed.

"If you change your mind! Call me," she replied.

I lifted my phone out of my pocket and texted Kamara as soon as I stepped off the elevator. I turned the corner and opened my condo door.

Me: Sorry about earlier.

My Baby: Are you all right?

Me: I fucked it up tonight.
My Baby: Can I come over?
Me: I'll call you tomorrow.
My Baby: Don't shut me out, D.
My Baby: I'm not, Kamara. I just need a minute.

I kicked off my shoes, placed my bag next to the door and went to the kitchen to grab a case of beer and drink the night away. I turned the TV onto FSNG and watched the response from the commentators.

My Baby: I'm here if you need me.

I didn't respond and just turned my phone off, kicked my feet up on the ottoman and sat in the chair as the highlights rolled.

"This was the worst performance of his career. The question is can he come back from this?" Ronnell sat on a panel with the usual crew of idiots that talk trash from Ben Simmons, Charles Adams, and Sean Camps.

"Listen, based on what I know and see he needs to just lay low and let someone fresh and new come in as quarterback," Ben said. I gulped down the first beer and popped a second open.

"I think he's at that age to possibly retire soon," Sean rebutted.

"Normally Ben I'd agree with you, but I think he had an off night," Charles rebutted.

"I doubt that Charles, you have a soft spot for the team. I'm telling you Julian is the one to watch. Besides, Donovan's too in love with that little writer. I mean the girl is so dowdy," Ben joked. They all laughed.

"I've heard she's some reporter in LA," Sean said.

"You have to give it to him. She's beautiful though," Ronnell said.

"Yeah, but she's a distraction, and it shows in the way he played tonight—and even at the National Championship before making it here. He was off, and I was the only one who told him to his face," Ben said.

"You did—and almost got knocked out tonight," Charles taunted.

I finished my beer and turned the TV off. I stood, dropping the bottle in the trash and going to the bedroom to pass out.

"Is she a distraction," I mumbled to myself and moved the pillow under my arms that Kamara used last time she was here. It still smelled like her as I dozed off to sleep.

* * *

Bang! Bang! Bang!

"Donovan Hunt open this door now!

Bang! Bang!

I turned in the bed, checked the time, and saw it was after nine in the morning. I rubbed my head and got out of bed and scratched my stomach and yawned.

"Donovan! Donovan!"

"Luna."

"You better open this door before I break it down," Luna yelled.

I came out of my room and walked down the staircase. I headed to the door and unlocked it to see Luna standing there with a harsh look on her face. She pushed me in the chest and shut the door.

"What are you doing here?"

"The question should be why are you acting like an ass to my best friend," Luna demanded.

I turned and walked off as she talked, and went to the kitchen to make some coffee before I got my day started.

"Luna are you really here to yell at me after what happened yesterday?" I picked up the coffee filter and poured water in the espresso machine and set the timer.

"If it makes you feel any better. Sorry about your game, now back to you hurting my friend," Luna said.

"I'll call her and apologize."

"Not good enough."

"Listen, I don't need you down my throat!" The timer went off and I poured the coffee and took a sip as I closed my eyes.

"Someone needs to remind you before you lose everything," Luna snapped.

"We're fine. I just need a few days to get my head clear."

"You did this back in college and cut everyone off for a few days when you lost some games. I thought you would have grown out of the pity party and manned up. It's a game, okay you lost one," Luna fussed, with her hands on her hips.

"Luna, not right now. I have enough from the reporters and sports analysts telling me how bad I fucked up; I don't need my sister coming in here to do the same."

"Then call your girlfriend and talk to her about your feelings." Luna picked up my cordless house phone and held it out for me. We had a stare off and I shook my head and walked out of the kitchen.

"Where are you going?" She extended her arm and turned me around to face her.

"I have work to do for a commercial shoot."

"Are you planning on reaching out to Kam today?"

"Drop it, Luna."

"If you fuck this up, don't blame this on me." Luna pointed in my face.

"Thanks for letting me know."

She waved me off and grabbed her purse to walk out of my apartment. I went back to my bedroom, jumped in the shower, and changed to get over to the location for the shoot that Sutton texted me a few days ago.

* * *

Two hours later I finally showed up. Even though I was late because of traffic, Sutton didn't take my excuses and reamed me out for the past twenty minutes.

"Do you know how bad this looks on me and my business?" Sutton complained.

"I said I was sorry, Sutton."

The wardrobe stylist double checked the shoes as I stood in front of a white backdrop with the logo of Millennium sports gear. I wore football gear from pants, shoes, and white t-shirt with their logo on the front.

"Your sorrys are getting real old, Donovan."

"Are you going to yell at me like Luna did?"

"Someone should, because you're pushing everyone away."

"The biggest game of my career and we lose. Sorry if I'm not in a fucking cheery mood."

"We get it, you didn't play your best, but that doesn't mean you take it out on the rest of the people that care about you," Sutton said.

"Have you talked to Paolo?"

"He emailed and asked if I could look into you doing an interview with Ben," Sutton said.

"That's not happening."

"We're all set to shoot," the director said. He brought in two women to stand beside me, wearing only bikini bottoms and sports bras with their logo on them.

"Let's get through this first and then we can worry about everything else later."

"How long is this going to take?" I asked.

"I don't know. Is there something more important you need to be doing?" Sutton huffed.

"What happened with Kaci?" I inquired, changing the subject.

"I fired her crazy ass. You should have told me she was coming on to you like that."

"I know, but you had a lot going on, and I got wrapped up in Kamara and the game, then I forgot."

"Kamara was the one that sent me the article," Sutton explained.

"Have you talked to her?"

"No, but we usually have dinner once a month," Sutton said.

"Mr. Hunt, I need you to just say the lines and look straight ahead," the director said.

A woman standing next to the camera held up white cards with writing and Sutton stepped out of the frame and watched.

"Action!" the director yelled.

"If you want to be like me, then Millennium Sports gear is what you need. Get into the gear," I said and looked at both women and smiled as they put their hands on the top of my shoulders and smiled at me. Then I glanced back at the camera and winked.

"Cut. One more take, make sure you pull them in close to you," the director explained.

I nodded, coughed, and started to do another take. This went on for seven hours, with different wardrobe changes throughout the day. They captured a few shots of me running in place, holding a football, and posing in the gear.

Once I finished for the day, I left and headed to Mickey's to grab something to eat. As soon as I made it to the restaurant, my phone rang, and I saw Paolo's name flash across the screen. It was going on five in the afternoon and I was beat for the day.

"Hey."

"You're a hard man to get a hold of, bro," Paolo said.

I opened the restaurant door and saw Mickey talking to a waitress. We made eye contact and nodded. I went to my usual spot.

"Sorry, had a long day at the shoot."

"Plus, a long night on the field."

"Savion told you."

"A little, sorry I missed the game. I had a family thing and flew out of town," Paolo stated.

The waitress came over and sat a menu down in front of me.

"Can I get a burger and fries, well done," I told her and she took the menu back and walked off to the kitchen.

"How is everything looking?"

"No matter what, you have two years left on your contract. They didn't like the way you handled yourself," Paolo explained.

"I know, fighting with my own team and coach."

"Plus punching a reporter."

"Ben's not a reporter; he's a scumbag."

"Doesn't matter, people listen to him and he brings in ratings."

"I'm not looking to be his best friend and go on his show."

"You should."

"Is this my agent talking or my best friend?"

"It's both, look Donovan, you look like a sore loser right now in the media and to your team."

"Ugh…" I ran a hand through my hair.

"Think about it and call me later on what you decide," Paolo said and hung up the phone.

I went to social media and saw what was being said about me.

@losangeleshawks: Donovan Hunt is making the team worse.

@HuntforLosangeles: I had an off night.

@JulianA: Donovan couldn't handle me or my team. LOL! He could learn some tips from me.

The comments went on and on to the point I was ready to step in and reply to them. But that would only make things worse for me and I didn't need the coach or management fining me for getting into fights online.

"I thought that was you sitting here." I looked up and saw Tabitha holding a shopping bag in her hand.

"You mind if I sit?" she asked.

"Sure."

"Thanks, it was a long day and I still have a lot more to do today," Tabitha said.

"What are you doing today?"

"I was helping my parents out by shopping for my sister's baby shower."

"I didn't know you had a sister," I said.

"Well, when we were together, we never really talked that much." She chuckled.

The waitress came back out with my Coke.

"Hi, I'm Samantha, can I get your order?" the waitress said. Tabitha looked at me for confirmation if she could eat with me and the place wasn't too crowded, and she wasn't annoying like usual, so I shrugged my shoulders giving her the okay.

"Can I get whatever he's having?"

"The burger and fries?" Samantha said.

"Yes please," Tabitha replied and Samantha strolled back to the kitchen to get her a drink.

"What's that look for?" I said as she grinned at me.

"You didn't kick me out."

"I've done enough damage with people."

"I understand, my parents reamed me out about the interview I did," Tabitha said.

"Why'd you do it?"

"You." Samantha came back to the booth and sat a Coke in front of Tabitha.

"What do you mean?"

"Thank you. Your rejection kind of bruised my ego," Tabitha said, pushing her straw into her cup.

"How many men have you been with since me?" I sat back in the booth and crossed my arms waiting for an answer.

"I'm not answering that question. How many women have you been with?" Tabitha argued.

"Not a lot, besides two or three here and there. Kamara's the most serious one though."

"I know."

I caught her looking sad at that comment.

"Tabitha we're having a decent conversation, let's not go back down memory lane."

"I promise I won't, but what is it about her that has you going crazy."

"She's simple."

"That's it."

"Unlike some women in my past, she doesn't try to impress me or be something she's not. I can talk with her about simple things and not feel like I need to be some bigtime athlete. I can just be Donovan," I said.

"I could do those things," Tabitha said. I tilted my head at her and curled my top lip.

She chortled and raised her hand, covering her mouth.

Samantha came back to our table and placed her food down.

"Okay, maybe I was a little conceited in the beginning. But I can change."

"That's the thing; I don't want you to change for me or anybody else. You have to want something more for yourself."

"You're right. I've been running behind you for so long trying to compete when we really aren't a good match for each other."

"So, you're going to stop doing these interviews?"

"Yes, it's not worth it honestly, Julian paid me to do them and say those things."

My eyes rose in shock.

"Explain that to me again?"

"Julian paid me to show up at Bar Cutz and those other places. He wanted to rattle your cage before the game."

"That son of a bitch."

"Sorry Donovan, I didn't think it would lead to us sitting here together actually having a conversation," Tabitha said.

"Yeah."

"Can we start over and be friends at least?" Tabitha asked.

"Friends only, nothing sexual," I responded and we clicked glasses together and talked for the rest of the afternoon about her sister's baby and her future plans of going back to school. After we finished eating and I paid for our food I walked her out of the restaurant and to her car when a photographer sitting in a car on the corner of the restaurant took photos of us.

"Damn, it never ends for you," Tabitha said and put her bags in the backseat.

"Not really, but at this point it's life until I retire."

"Go make up with your girl and tell her this business

can be rough and manipulative," Tabitha said. She reached over and gave me a hug as more cameras clicked.

I flipped them off and watched as she got in her car and pulled off. I left to talk to Savion about the interview idea before going to talk with Kamara and apologize.

Flashback Night of the Big Game.

Donovan didn't answer my calls as Savion's car pulled off to drive him home. I knew he was pissed off after losing the game, but pushing everyone away isn't the answer. I dialed his number again, and it went straight to voicemail.

"Ugh!" I huffed and stuck the phone in my purse.

"Kamara, it's getting late. You need us to take you home?" Dad asked.

"No, I brought my car. I'm going to head over to Donovan's to check on him," I answered.

"Are you sure? He might not want any company, baby," Dad replied.

"I won't stay long. I'm sorry your first box-seat game didn't end the way you wanted." I kissed him on the cheek, and he rubbed a hand across my back.

Luna walked over toward me, with her parents behind her.

"Bestie, I'm heading home. Donovan's going to be on a kick for a little bit," Luna said.

"What do you mean?"

"Whenever he loses my brother gets into a mood of shutting

us out and not wanting to be bothered. It'll blow over in a few days," Luna replied.

I nodded feeling a knot in my stomach at Donovan shutting me out and going cold. We've pretty much been around each other nonstop since we became a couple and now to not hear from him or see his smile will completely rip me apart. I've never given myself to someone this deep and fully.

"Thanks for letting me know," I said. All three of them hugged me and walked off to her car and left. I rubbed my hands together nervously praying he wasn't so upset that he wouldn't speak to me since it wasn't so late.

* * *

FORTY MINUTES later after driving to his condo, I pulled up to the building and tried texting him.

Me: Hey, I'm here, outside your building.

Donovan didn't text me back, so I tried again.

Me: Donovan, are you home?

Donovan: I'm not in the mood for company.

Me: I understand but talking about it would help.

Donovan: When I'm in the right headspace, I'll contact you.

I was growing increasingly frustrated, so I jumped out of the car and went inside of the building and tried to walk toward the elevator, but the receptionist stopped me.

"Hello, can I help you?" The receptionist went back and forth with Sutton a few weeks back.

"I'm going upstairs."

"You don't live in this building," she said.

"My boyfriend does."

"Who's your boyfriend?" she questioned.

I cocked my head to the side with my hand on my hip.

"You know who my boyfriend is. Donovan Hunt."

"Well, Mr. Hunt isn't taking any visitors right now."

Her eyes looked me up and down, like she was trying to assess what Donovan saw in me—kind of like the rest of the world. I knew we were polar opposites: I was more of a homebody, just a writer, trying to make things better for the average person; he was a big, jock millionaire with all these fans and celebrities who wanted to be his friend.

"Did he say that?" I wondered, as I crossed my arms over my chest.

"As a matter of fact, he did. No visitors for the rest of the night." She winked and walked around me to head back to the desk.

I rolled my eyes, looked over at the elevator, and went back to my car, then drove back home.

The next day I was in the office, reading over the latest reviews of the piece I did on the business district that the local government was trying to dismantle. I still hadn't talked to Donovan, and I was getting more pissed by the minute that he never answered the phone for me and had totally cut me off.

Cailey walked in and pointed toward the sales figures for the newspaper. "Great numbers, Kamara. I think you should go to the hearing."

"What hearing?"

"The mayor saw your piece and wanted to know what's going on out there," Cailey said.

"Really?"

"We might be able to swing an interview."

"You think he'd sit down with me?"

"Probably, but he'd like to have Donovan do an endorsement for him as a thank you," Cailey blurted out.

"So, he's only interested in talking with me if my boyfriend comes?"

"Think of it as a favor for a favor. If he can bring awareness to your friend's business that's a good thing," Cailey answered.

"Yeah, but I would be using Donovan and right now we're not on speaking terms."

"I know he lost the game last night."

A knock came at the door and I looked up to see Luna stroll inside.

"Cailey, I left a new article on your desk," Luna said and took a seat atop my desk.

"Good because you've been slacking," Cailey said.

Cailey stood and tapped the documents on top of my desk that she dropped off and glanced up at me.

"Think about this and get back to me," Cailey said and walked out.

"What's wrong?" Luna questioned.

"Have you talked to your brother?" I asked.

"Yeah, he's an idiot."

"He's avoiding my calls."

"Donovan is just going through the normal thing that athletes go through," Luna remarked. I continued researching over what I could find about the upcoming hearing at the City Council board meeting as Luna talked about her latest dating issues.

"I'm tired of all of these guys that keep wanting to get serious," Luna said.

"What's wrong with that?"

"Kamara, I'm too young to settle down. You should be out there dating more than one guy."

"I might be doing that soon," I mumbled to myself.

"If it makes you feel any better, I yelled at him about you."

"Thanks, but I don't want you getting in the middle of something that would hurt your relationship. I'm fine."

"How about tonight we have a girls' night and watch

movies in our pajamas and eat popcorn, drink wine, and have ice cream?" Luna asked.

"I thought you had a date."

"It can wait. Besides, you're more important," Luna said.

"No, don't change your plans because of me. I have too much work to do here anyway," I said.

She understood and left my office. For the rest of the day, I focused on what I could control—my work. I threw myself into the job.

Once everyone left for the day, I yawned and noticed it was going on eight at night, and I'd been at the office since eight that morning. I packed up the rest of my work and went home to curl up in bed and watch my favorite movie, *Coming to America*, for the hundredth time.

A week later, I was sitting in the back of the room, watching as people went back and forth, debating whether it was a good idea to push all the local businesses out of the area. Abigail was there, along with Terry, who had surprisingly come to support me. He told me that most of the homeless would end up having to move out of the area if this passed.

"I own the local clothing store in the area, and this would destroy my business," said an older woman, standing with a younger girl next to her. They looked alike so more than likely, she was her daughter or niece.

Earlier, a few people had started talking about why the mayor wasn't there when he was requested. I asked Cailey when I started the story how deep I could go and whether she'd support me. So far, things had erupted to all-out protests.

"We demand you vote to oppose this now!" the woman said.

"Thank you for your information. As the council members on the board, we have to do what's best for the businesses and the community. As of now, this is up for debate and we'll hold a vote," Chairman Dewin said.

"That's not good enough!" a guy stood and shouted, holding a sign that read: *We aren't moving.* Earlier, he'd spoken about his record store, which was in the middle of the mall blueprints.

"This is getting out of hand," Abigail whispered to me.

I had my notepad out to keep updated on everything that was said for my article.

"What happened to Rodney? I thought he was coming today," I said.

"I told him to stay behind and watch the shop," Abigail explained.

"We're going to hear everyone out, but we need order," Chairman Dewin said.

"I can't believe they're seriously going through with this," I muttered.

"I can. The council is only out for money. Forget the rest of us little people," Abigail announced.

I nodded.

The chairman spoke again, and a few minutes later, they dismissed everyone for the day, saying that they would reconvene in a day or two. I had enough for my follow-up article, but I wanted to try to get the mayor on record if possible. I stood and turned to leave, with Abigail and Terry next to me.

"Terry, what are you going to do if they vote to approve?" I asked.

"I'll need to find another place to stay," Terry responded.

"Maybe the shelters have space for you," Abigail said, pushing the front door of the Capitol Building open.

We stepped outside to a massive group of reporters and

photographers. All of them rushed toward us and stuck microphones in my face.

"Kamara are you still dating Donovan Hunt?" a reporter asked.

"No comment." I knew how these guys could twist anything you say.

"We have him out on a date with an ex. Sure *looks* like he moved on," another guy brought up.

I didn't know what he was talking about. He shoved his phone in my face. I saw a photo of Donovan, smiling with that Tabitha lady from the grocery store, and my face couldn't hide how I was feeling.

"She said, 'No comment,'" Abigail said and pushed them away to get us to her car. I'd driven in with her today and left my car at the newspaper.

"He's the highest paid player in the league, you can't expect him to be a one-woman guy," a female reporter said, smirking.

"How about you report on the real issues in the world, and not someone's love life?" I shot back and got inside Abigail's car.

That only made them even hungrier for more because they swarmed her car and threw question after question at me about his performance at the big game and made comments about how men like him couldn't commit. I pulled my phone out and went to social media, and I saw some people had tagged me in photos of him out with other women, but they seemed like older pictures because he had blond hair back then.

Abigail pulled off into traffic, and I sat staring out the window. I hadn't talked to him since the night of the game, and I was waiting for him to get in touch with me. I knew he was feeling bad about losing the game—especially to

Julian—but to cut me off and go cold was a new low that I hadn't expected.

"Ignore those reporters Kam, they're just trying to get you riled up," Abigail said.

"He texted me last night that he was coming over but never came. Now I see why."

"We're going to drop Terry off and go out tonight," Abigail said.

"I have too much work to do, Abigail."

"Forget work and forget him, tonight is all about you having a ladies' night with your girls. Call up Luna and Sutton."

"I don't know if that's a good idea."

"Why not?"

"For one, Luna's his sister, and Sutton's his publicist."

"So, they're still your friends first and foremost." Abigail pulled over to the front of her coffee shop and let Terry out.

"They are, but I don't want it to be awkward with us."

"It won't be."

"Text them and see," Abigail said.

I grabbed my phone out of my pocket and texted them both in a group message.

Me: I need a night out.

Luna: Strip club?

Sutton: I'm down.

Me: I was thinking of a regular club.

Sutton: We can go back to the club we went to last time.

Luna: Are you sure about this, Kam? A lot of celebrities and photographers hang out there.

Me: I'll be fine.

Sutton: I saw him yesterday.

Luna: I told him he fucked up.

Me: Let's not talk about him for the night. Abigail is coming.

Sutton: He said he was going to call you.
Me: He lied and was out with another woman.
Luna: I'm kicking his ass.
Sutton: What woman?
Me: Not important.
Luna: Meet us at the club. I'll get us a booth in VIP.

I closed off my messages and sat back in the car as she drove to my place to change.

"Once you get your head full of alcohol and relax, you'll forget about your troubles."

"Let's hope so."

TWO HOURS LATER, I was drinking and dancing next to Luna in the VIP section. Whatever was in the drink she bought me was doing its job and helping me forget all my worries. I took another sip and waved for the bottle girl to bring me two more. I'd decided to let loose tonight and let my hair down. I was wearing a red halter top, black leather shorts, and knee-high boots. It was appropriate for the way I was feeling—hot from dancing and drinking. The DJ dropped the newest Rihanna song, and all four of us got up, snapping our fingers.

"Let's go downstairs to the dance floor." Luna had her hair in a ponytail, and she wore red lipstick and a short gold off the shoulder dress and Sutton had on a leopard catsuit with a V-neck that stopped at her belly button.

"I plan on taking somebody home tonight," Abigail sang, twisting her hips from side to side. She was wearing a long black dress with a split on the side, and her hair was straightened with a part down the middle.

"Show us what you got, Kam," Luna called out, booty bumping me.

I laughed and bumped her back, then started popping my hips and moving my hands up and down my body. Luna, Sutton, and Abigail cheered me on and moved with the beat of the song. They joined me as we became the stars of the dance floor. After three more songs, they started to walk off, but I kept going.

"Keep moving your hips like that and you'll make a man worship at your feet." I heard a voice speak in my ear. I giggled and felt his arms around my waist.

"What's your name, sexy?"

"Kamara. What's yours?"

"Julian."

He spoke and I froze, then turned in his arms. He smirked.

"I'm actually done with dancing."

"Come on Kamara, this doesn't have to be awkward."

"It does because you don't know how to keep your mouth shut."

"Damn, baby you hurt my feelings."

"You have feelings?" I questioned and he tightened his hold around me.

"I can have whatever you want me to have, sweetheart." He kissed the side of my cheek and all of a sudden I felt myself being yanked backwards.

"OMG!" I almost fell on the ground, but someone caught me, and I looked up to see Reuben. Which only meant Donovan was the one that yanked me.

"What the hell do you think you're doing!" Donovan shouted.

"I'm dancing with my date," Julian lied and I looked at him perplexed.

"You're on a date with him?" Donovan asked me and I opened my mouth to speak and I got stuck.

"She is and we were having a good time before you

interrupted," Julian said. I got out of Reuben's arms and marched back over to them.

"Donovan, I haven't spoken to you since the night of the game. You have no right asking me who I'm dancing with."

"Kamara stay out of this," Donovan demanded.

"Kamara let's go back to my section so we can finish that talk about our night cap," Julian lied again, and Donovan pushed me behind him and punched Julian in the face.

"Donovan, no! Reuben, do something!" I screamed, trying to break them up, but Reuben stood back and crossed his arms, ready for Julian's friends to try and jump in. I dropped my head into my hands. "Where is Savion?!" I yelled and went to pull Donovan back. He jerked out of my hold. "Donovan, stop this mess!"

"Get the fuck back!" he shouted, and I jumped, frightened at the look in his eyes. I knew he wouldn't hit me or anything, but he wasn't the Donovan I knew that was funny, sweet, and caring.

"You know what? I don't even care," I said and started to walk away.

They threw punches back and forth.

The DJ had already stopped the music, and security was coming over to calm everyone down.

I walked over to our booth and grabbed my purse. Luna and Sutton were not there, and I saw Abigail talking with some guy.

"Abigail I'm leaving."

"Why? What happened?" Abigail asked, jumping up.

"Ask your friend down there." I pointed to Donovan and Julian held back by security yelling at each other.

"Let me take you home," Abigail said.

"No, you stay, and I'll catch a cab."

"I'm not letting you catch a cab this late."

"Are you sure?"

"Yes. Let me tell him I'm leaving. Meet me out front," Abigail said.

I started to walk out of the section and downstairs past the chaos when I saw Luna and Sutton, trying to calm Donovan down.

"Kamara! Kamara!" I heard my name being called, but I ignored them and stood outside of the club. I started to walk toward Abigail's car when a flash of light was in my face.

"Kamara! Over here, Kamara!" a guy screamed and I pushed his camera out of my face.

"Leave me alone!" I screamed.

"Did you sleep with Julian to get back at Donovan?" A question was thrown at me and I balled my fist up ready to knock the camera out of his hand.

"Kamara, here's your chance. Tell the people how you're dating two rival players?" he asked, and I started to speak when I felt a presence from behind.

"Kamara get in my car," Donovan said.

"I'm riding with Abigail."

"Is this a lovers' squabble? Donovan, how do you feel about your ex sleeping with Julian?" The guy pushed the camera in Donovan's face. He lunged for him.

I yelled out, "Donovan, no! Take me home now."

He glared at the camera guy and looked back at me and grabbed my hand, went to his car, and opened the passenger door to let me in as Luna, Abigail, and Sutton came out finally.

"Mara we can drop you off," Luna said.

"She's riding with me," Donovan said.

"Are you sure, Mara?" Luna questioned and I smiled appreciating my friend had my back.

"I'll be fine."

"Okay, call me when you make it inside," Luna told me and gave her brother a harsh grimace.

Donovan started the car and pulled out of the parking structure, then drove off, not saying a word. I couldn't believe the way the night had gone, and how he'd acted in front of everyone. I was beyond embarrassed and pissed that I'd let myself get so involved in his mess with Julian. I'd been used as a pawn.

Fifteen minutes later, we pulled up to his place, and I was ready to just completely lose it altogether.

"This isn't my apartment."

"Get out," Donovan said.

"You were supposed to take me home."

"This *is* your home," he stated. He walked around to the passenger side and opened the door.

I peered at him, waiting to see if he was serious. He didn't flinch. I jumped out of his car and strolled up to his condo without a word. I'd call a cab.

Bypassing the security guard, we made it into the elevator and to his front door a few minutes later. He slid the key into the lock, and I walked in and sat on the couch. I pulled my phone out of my purse to make a call. I started to dial, but he snatched it out of my hand.

"Give me my phone, Donovan."

"Talk to me."

He put my phone in his pocket.

"Now you want to talk? You're ridiculous."

Donovan sighed and walked up close to me and placed his hands on my hips.

"I apologize for not making things right."

"You ignored me and went cold for two weeks."

"I know, baby." He bent down and kissed me on the

forehead, then on my cheek, then buried his face against my neck.

"No, that won't work this time." I stepped out of his grasp.

"What can I say to make it right?"

"Are you back sleeping with Tabitha?"

"No of course not."

"How do I know that? I haven't seen or spoken to you in two weeks!"

He crashed his lips against mine. Soon, I got lost in the feeling of his large hands cupping my ass, and the smell of his smoky sage cologne.

"No, wait Donovan." I finally got enough strength to push him back.

"I'm sorry, Mara. Forgive me, please," Donovan begged, grasping my chin. He bent down and captured my lips again. His hands slid down my arms toward my back. The minute we locked in a tight embrace I felt his growing manhood against my leg. Not only had I been missing our talks and funny banter, but also our long nights of love-making and feeling him inside me.

"Take this off." Donovan's voice was filled with lust and urgency.

I was taking too long to get undressed. He dropped to his knees, ripped my shorts and panties off, and pushed me against the wall. He lifted my leg over his shoulder and spread open my entrance, swiping his tongue against my clit. I buckled at the knees, almost falling, gripping his shoulders to stay upright as we peered at each other. Something in his eyes was asking for permission and wanted me to forgive him for the way he'd treated me.

"Can I make it up to you, baby?" Donovan trailed kisses down my thighs, caressing me with both hands.

"Yes…" I whimpered, stripping out of my red halter top.

Donovan stood and removed his shirt, pants, and shoes, then carried me to the bathroom. He put me down and turned the shower on, then extended his hand for me to take. He gripped me tight in his arms and nuzzled his face against my neck.

"I'm an idiot for shutting you out," Donovan said, pulling back and cupping both sides of my face.

"I agree."

He smirked, opening the shower door farther and letting me in first to step under the water. It was a luxurious, spa-like, stainless-steel shower with dual showerheads, a bench in the corner, and a mosaic-tiled floor. Donovan gently massaged one of my breasts with one hand and put his lips on the other.

"Ohhh…"

Feeling the bliss that was coming from the strokes of his tongue and hand, I pressed a hand against his large girth and started stroking him.

"I want to please you all night baby and show you how sorry I am." Donovan bit gently on my nipple, then flicked his tongue across it. They grew harder at his familiar touch, a pool of moisture seeping down my thigh.

"Turn around, place your hands flat on the wall," he demanded, and I stood on my tiptoes to peck his lips and turned around facing the bench with my hands on the wall and legs spread.

"Ahhh!"

"Just like I remembered," Donovan muttered as he spread my ass cheeks wide and spit, inserted his index finger and pumped in and out as his tongue was buried deep in my backdoor.

"Oh God! Donovan," I screeched, feeling the double penetration. Donovan was the most adventurous lover I'd ever had and the things he'd done to my body only made me want him more and more. Hearing his moans of passion took me to the edge and I wanted to feel his dick.

"I... I... can't," I rushed out, feeling my legs getting weak. Not only dealing with the steamy hot water, but his skills was making it hard to even remember why we haven't talked in a couple of weeks. All of a sudden I felt Donovan poking my entrance. He eased in slowly as he kissed the top of my shoulder. The both of us sighed in relief.

"Shit... baby, you take my breath away," Donovan remarked, sliding out and turning me around. He changed positions, sitting on the bench.

I straddled his lap and gripped his dick, positioning him at my entrance and lowering myself slowly. I wrapped my arms around his neck. As he pumped upward, I met his thrusts.

"I love you Mara baby." Donovan kissed along my jaw, neck, chin, then captured my lips and eased his tongue inside. We went for two more rounds until the water turned cold and eventually cleaned ourselves off and got into bed together wrapped up in each other's arms.

"I love you, too."

*D*uring the early morning, I eased out of Donovan's arms and left a note on his pillow.

I didn't want to wake you, but I needed to clear my head.

I don't think sex would help without really talking about how things happened.

—Kamara

Since then, I've been working in Cafe Sin all morning drinking coffee and talking with Abigail about what happened. Donovan and Luna have called me nonstop all morning and I haven't returned a message.

"What do you plan on saying?" Abigail asked as she placed another vanilla latte in front of me. I cut off a piece of the banana muffin and tossed it in my mouth. I was waiting on Luna to meet up with me for a girls' night later today and movies.

"I have no idea, he basically brought me back to his condo and we-"

"No reason to go any further." She giggled, standing next to the chair.

"Well, I won't be one of those girls that lets him get

away with just dropping me off like a toy when he feels like it."

"Hopefully, you two can work it out."

"We'll see. But have you heard from the mayor or the board about the vote?" I asked.

"We received a letter in the mail about the board not moving forward with the vote. So, we can keep our shop thank God," Abigail said.

"I didn't think I'd see you again," he said.

I looked up, no longer smiling.

Abigail pointed. "Aren't you the guy from the club?"

"Julian Anderson." He extended his palm for a shake.

"The guy who went on TV and talked about my friend Donovan," Abigail said.

Julian's smile dropped.

"I need to finish putting in my inventory. Call me if you need me, Mara," Abigail said and walked off. Julian took a seat across from me at the table.

"What?"

"Go out with me?" Julian asked.

"No."

"Why not?"

"Because I have more than enough drama from one football player. I don't need any more excuses to have the public in my life," I explained, turning to type on my computer.

"I saw the interview you did with Donovan. I'd like to do one with you," Julian said.

"What are you trying to do?" I inquired.

He leaned back in the chair.

"This would be good for your career to have an interview with me," Julian told me, gassing himself up.

"I don't need an interview with you. I'm happy where I am in my career."

"Are you fucking kidding me?!" a familiar voice shouted.

I looked over Julian's shoulder. Donovan was standing with Savion.

"Donovan."

"I thought we cleared things yesterday Kamara, you're out with my enemy now," Donovan said.

"Is this your boyfriend? I wouldn't have asked you out on a date if I knew that," Julian said, playing games.

Donovan's nostrils flared, and he lunged at Julian.

I jumped back.

"Donovan no!" I screamed as he punched Julian in the face.

Julian wiped the side of his mouth as the blood dripped and sent a hit back to Donovan.

"That's enough, Donovan. This wouldn't have happened if you were honest with me."

"Bro, calm down," Savion said.

"I could sue your ass for this," Julian taunted.

Abigail came over with a broom.

"Let's go, Kamara," Donovan said.

"I'm not going anywhere with you."

"She's agreed to do an interview with me. You're not the only one that Kamara can write about," Julian egged on.

"Stop lying, Julian, and go, please," I said.

Julian shook his head, pulling his phone out of his pocket.

"At least take my number. I'm serious about the interview," Julian said.

Donovan glared at me.

I was still wondering whether I should pursue the opportunity or not.

"Kamara," Donovan called my name and I bent down to grab my bag and computer to walk out.

"Sorry, Abigail," I said and walked out of the shop as Donovan followed me.

I saw Terry at the bus stop bench and wanted to check in on him, but I was over the stress of the day. I went to my car door, opened it, and tossed everything inside.

"Can you talk to me please?" Donovan said.

"When I'm ready to talk I'll call you."

I started the car and drove off leaving him in my rearview mirror standing with his head down in misery.

"Serves him right."

* * *

Forty minutes later I pulled up to my parents' house and walked inside and fell face first on the couch. My mother came into the living room wearing a robe.

"Hey baby," Mom said.

"Hi," I mumbled into the pillow.

She sat on the edge of the couch.

"What's wrong with you?"

"Men."

"Donovan, I take it?" she asked.

"Where's Dad?" I questioned.

"He went to the store to grab some groceries."

"Why aren't you at work?" I asked, checking the time on my watch showing one pm.

"I took a personal day," Mom said.

"Is everything all right?"

"Yeah, talk to me. You don't look like my normal bubbly daughter." Mom rubbed my forehead to check my temperature.

"I'm not sick." I sat up on the couch, legs underneath me.

"So, what happened with Donovan?"

"We haven't spoken since the game that he lost. All he did was ignore me for two weeks—and it probably would have been more."

"You know men have fragile egos, baby," Mom said.

"I know, so he comes to the club and breaks up my girls' night and I end up going back home with him."

"Okay."

"He thought he could just apologize and that would be it."

"What else happened?" she probed.

"I slept with him." I dropped my face in my hands.

"Hmm."

I looked up at her.

"You think I'm being too soft with him?"

"That's not for me to decide, baby. If you feel like that wasn't enough, then it's up to you to define what boundaries he crossed and let him fix them. But you can't hold it against him forever," Mom explained.

The front door opened, and my Dad strolled in with two bags of groceries.

"I thought that was your car out there," Dad said, bending down to kiss me on the forehead.

"Your daughter needed some relationship advice," Mom said.

"Tell me you're not letting that boy dog you out?" Dad argued.

"No. It's complicated. I shouldn't have come," I said.

"She'll be fine, put the groceries away, baby," Mom told my Dad.

He grunted and left the room. We giggled at his attitude.

"Don't have your Dad ready to fight that boy," Mom said and I nodded.

"Maybe I need to explore being single again."

"Maybe."

"Mom, you're no help."

"Baby, you're grown. I taught you to define yourself and never let anyone do it for you. Put your foot down and let him know," Mom said.

"You're right." I jumped up and hugged her.

"I know I am. Now, get out of my house because I'm about to have a date with your father," Mom explained. I rolled my eyes, and she winked at me.

* * *

I POPPED the bottle of wine Luna brought over and poured a glass for us. Sutton was in charge of bringing dinner, Luna was in charge of the wine, Abigail was in charge of snacks, and I already had the movies. After I left my parents' house, I wanted to be stuck in the house for the rest of the night and just get drunk with my friends and pig out on food. Sutton brought over a mixture of all my favorite meals, including pizza, sub sandwiches, Chinese food, and burgers.

"Did you get hot wings?" Luna asked as she licked the ketchup from her finger. I passed each of us a glass of wine and sat on the floor as Coming to America started to play.

"So, what happened after Kam left Abigail?" Sutton asked.

Abigail took a slice of pizza and egg roll on a plate, as I grabbed a mixture of fries and orange chicken and rice.

"Savion basically told Julian to stay away from you," Abigail said.

"She's grown, she can talk to any guy she wants," Luna remarked.

"I would normally agree with you Luna, but this is Donovan's enemy," Sutton said.

"OMG! This is not war, Sutton. It's football," Luna fussed.

"Yeah, football and your brother is crazy. I'm surprised he's not on the blogs yet. I've been checking ever since Savion called me about what happened," Sutton explained, showing her phone to us.

"What's going on with you and Savion?" I questioned, lifting my glass of wine.

"We're just friends." Sutton shrugged.

"Friends that like to suck—" Luna blurted out.

Sutton threw a pillow at Luna.

Luna chuckled at the pout on Sutton's lip.

"You're not innocent either, Luna," I said.

"I admit I freely love," Luna said.

"The question is who this week is receiving that love," Sutton replied.

Luna pressed her finger to the side of her cheek in thought.

"Jerry this week and Cory in two weeks," Luna responded and I smirked.

"Tonight it's about Kamara, drowning her sorrows in junk food, watching her favorite films, and avoiding all talk of Donovan," Abigail said.

I lay my head on the edge of the couch, thinking about Donovan. I still couldn't get the look in his eyes out of my head. If I allowed what happened the other night to happen again, then he would think I was a pushover.

"Listen, I love my brother, but you have to do what makes you happy, Kamara," Luna said.

"Are you going to do the interview with Julian?" Abigail asked.

Sutton spit her food at that statement.

"What interview?" Sutton said.

"He asked me at the shop to do an interview with him. I think it was to just mess with Donovan."

"He's trying to use you Kam, don't feed into his games. Julian's a bigger jerk than Donovan," Sutton said.

"I know, it's obvious what he's trying to do, but I have enough to deal with."

"Besides, you're on a career path without having to sink to his level," Luna said.

The movie came on at the favorite part of them in the barber shop. We laughed and continued on for the evening as my phone rang and a knock came at the door.

"Who can that be?" Sutton said.

"I don't know." I put my plate down on the table and stood still holding my phone, opening the door.

"Can we talk?" Donovan said.

"I'm not ready to talk, Donovan."

I crossed my arms over my chest.

"Donovan? What are you doing?" Luna said.

"Luna, talk to your friend and tell her I'm sorry for being an ass." He leaned against the front door.

"Luna can't convince me of you being sorry. That's my determination based on your actions, Donovan."

"Then give me a chance to make it up, Mara."

"I'll think about it and you might want to try starting with not coming on to your ex," I said and slammed the door in his face.

"I guess she told him," Abigail said.

I placed my phone on do not disturb and finished eating. We watched movies until I passed out later that night. Sutton and Abigail went home, while Luna spent the night.

Two days later, I felt Mara was taking this situation too far, and I was getting increasingly aggravated that Julian was on social media, basically talking about how he stole my girl. Even having him in her presence at the shop did something to me, and I felt the urge to hammer his face in even more than I had that afternoon.

"Remember to stay calm, Donovan. I don't need you acting out of character," Sutton explained. She'd set up an interview for me with FSNG Sports to discuss the rumors, and my plans for the future.

I was determined to get through this without breaking someone's face, but I couldn't guarantee that wouldn't happen.

"I wish you were this helpful when I went to see Mara," I huffed, walked out to the set of the show, and took a seat. Sutton rolled her eyes and stood next to the camera and makeup artist.

"Mr. Hunt it's a pleasure to have you with us," Ben said, tauntingly.

"I noticed."

The director motioned for the on-air sign and Ben nodded and prepared to speak.

"Ladies and gentlemen, I have an exclusive interview with the man himself. Mr. Donovan Hunt, the MVP, game winning champion has agreed to sit with me to talk."

I smiled for the camera.

"Donovan let's start with the rumors that you've broken up with your girlfriend."

"You can call me Mr. Hunt."

He chuckled.

"First thought when you lost the big game that night?"

"I was disappointed like anyone on my team."

"Do you think you overplayed your hand? I mean you've given off the I'm the best at this and the only person that can win status."

"Is that why you've had it out for me?"

"Aw, did I hurt your feelings? I like to speak the truth."

"Truth or lies? Because all my teammates know that Julian talks a good game, but he's not the one who brought a game-winning ring home," I said.

"You have to admit that the drug accusations are pretty out there," Ben said.

"That's the problem with the media. You paint this narrative, and once it gets out and fan the flames, you can't contain what you started," I explained.

"Well, we have to take a break, and we'll be right back," Ben said.

"Ben you have ten more minutes then we have to leave," Sutton explained.

"All I need is five," Ben replied.

The cameras started rolling again.

"Sports talk, we are back. I'm your host Ben Simmons

and today we have Donovan Hunt of the Los Angeles Hawks."

Sutton gave me her thumbs up.

"Mr. Hunt are you sleeping with Tabitha, your old girlfriend again?"

"No, and to add on Tabitha was never my girlfriend."

"She's what you celebrities call booty calls?" Ben asked.

"See, now you're being disrespectful."

Ben held his hands up, backing down.

"She was a close friend?" he questioned.

"Yes."

"What about your publicist's assistant Kaci and the writer Kamara Powell?" Ben asked.

"You seem to be obsessed with my life. What's the point?"

"As public figures we have the right to know who the role models are and the one's that influence and give our kids a bad impression," Ben explained.

"I never said I was a role model, and I don't want that label put on me. I don't talk about my love life."

"Then it goes back to why did you drop the ball? Drugs? Girlfriend problems?" Ben questioned.

"One of the moments where I didn't play well. That's it."

Ben held the cliff notes in his hand and faced the camera.

"Ladies and gentlemen, that's all I have for today. Continue to stay in the know and follow the 'Ben Simmons Show' for all the juicy gossip," Ben announced, then reached over to give me a handshake.

"I only report factual statements and my sources are cleared," Ben said.

"No, you report lies Mr. Simmons, let's not pretend you're doing me a favor here."

Ben shifted in his seat.

"All of what you've said could be true, but my audience understands what I do here."

"Yeah, you spill lies and give the wrong people a platform. I never said I should be given the golden ticket. I worked hard for my position," I argued.

"Thanks for your time, Ben. We have to go," Sutton said.

I stood, ripped off the microphone, and stormed out of the show. My mind wasn't in the right headspace to do this interview because of everything going on with Kamara. I opened the passenger side door for Sutton, and she slid in. I walked around to the driver's side, jumped in, and started the car.

"That was uncalled for Donovan," Sutton complained.

"What did you want me to do?"

"I wanted you to be calm and act like you have some sense in there."

I drove down the Santa Monica Blvd. away from Sunset Gower studios to head back on the freeway to her office.

"He's a freaking idiot and you know that, Sutton."

"I don't disagree, but you need to get that stick out of your ass."

"How's Kamara?"

"She's working Donovan and you need to figure out how to fix this."

"She's not talking to me."

"Because you went on a date with another woman."

"I didn't go on a date. I was out eating, and she showed up. It's not a big deal," I said.

"Whatever it was; you shouldn't have hugged her."

I ran a hand down my face.

"Kamara needs to know that you're not going to shut her out again."

"How do I do that?"

She leaned over and tapped me on the chest.

"You're a big boy, you'll figure it out."

I turned off the freeway and pulled up to her office and she stepped out and leaned in the window.

"Remember you were in the wrong and you need to beg for forgiveness."

"Is this how you treat my boy Savion?"

"Savion's not stupid enough to screw up like you." She grinned and stood, heading into her building.

I waited for her to get in before pulling off to head to the gym and work out some aggression. I parked at the private gym reserved for athletes, got out, picked up my bag, and walked inside. I lifted my head to see Josh, the gym manager.

"You look like shit," Josh said.

I placed the bag on top of the counter.

"What's it looking like in here today?"

"Not busy. A few guys are here. I think Savion's in the back."

"Cool, let me get in here to work off some stress."

"I didn't get to tell you but don't let these media folks get to you," Josh said.

"Thanks." We slapped hands and I walked off to head to the back, dropped my bag in the locker room cage and changed into shorts and a gym shirt. I walked out with a towel wrapped around my neck, a bottle of water and went to the weight machine next to Savion. I lifted the weights and dropped the water and towel on the ground.

"Sutton said you fucked up the interview," Savion said.

"I wouldn't call it fucked up."

"She said you looked like you might hit Ben on camera."

I lifted the 50-pound weight to my chest, then back

down four times. I looked over at Savion and dropped the weight down on the stanchion.

"Has Kamara contacted you yet?"

"No and that shit is pissing me off."

"That's what women do," Savion said.

"She saw a photo of me and Tabitha together."

"Wait, your back with Tabitha?" he asked.

"Hell no, she saw me out having lunch and apologized for the bullshit she did in that interview."

"Damn."

"Yeah."

"If the interview comes out like I think it did you need to do more than apologize to Kamara."

"That bullshit was stupid, and I played right into his hands."

"Don't beat yourself up, maybe they'll go easy on you," Savion joked.

"You think she'll take me back?"

"Kamara loves you; I can see it in her eyes. Why don't we go out for drinks at the bar?"

"I'm heading home after this and figuring out how to get my girl."

"Good answer," Savion said.

"I know one thing. If Julian tries another thing, I'm kicking his ass."

"Don't get into trouble with the cops. You remember that one time you got arrested at a bar for fighting."

"That wasn't my fault he thought he could challenge me."

"That's the problem now. Sutton is trying to keep your reputation under control."

"I wouldn't have these problems if you and Reuben would stop bringing me into your shit," I fussed.

"Hold yourself accountable, bro," Savion said, and I flipped him off.

The rest of the time we went back and forth discussing the new strategy of plays and getting back into the new season of football. After the workout I drove home, showered, and ordered food and watched a replay of the game.

* * *

I FELL asleep on the couch, after a food coma and thought I heard Kamara calling my name. I tossed and turned, finally opening my eyes when I heard loud knocking on my door.

"Kamara," I muttered, jumped up, looked around my living room and checked the time on my AP and wiped my eyes.

"Donovan! It's me."

I rose and walked to the door and opened it to see Kamara standing soaking wet.

"Can I come inside?" she asked. I stood to the side to let her in and shut the door.

"What are you doing here?" I asked as I headed to the bathroom and grabbed a towel for her to dry off with.

"I wanted to talk to you."

"You could have waited. You're going to catch a cold or something." I rubbed her shoulders, then down her arms.

"Let me grab you something to change into. You'll catch pneumonia."

"Wait, let me say this first." Kamara gripped my arm.

I turned.

"What?"

"The only way we can get back on track is if you're honest with me."

"I agree."

"Then can I have a seat?" she asked.

"You don't have to ask that, Mara."

"Thanks."

"Did you go out with Julian?" I queried.

"No, but I might do the interview with him and I wanted to know how you feel about that."

"That's your job. I can't dictate what you love, and I wouldn't want to. Is he my favorite person? No."

"I saw a clip of your interview."

"How did you see it so early?"

"Sutton got an early copy."

"She's pissed I lost my cool earlier."

"I don't blame her. You need to do better and play nice," she teased, placed the towel down on the couch and sat. I sat across from her and crossed my arms.

"Does that mean you forgive me?"

"Yes, I forgive you. But this can't happen again, Donovan. I take trust very seriously and you hurt me."

"I know, Mara." I went to sit, but she held a hand up.

"Shutting me out and then trying to come back and act like fucking me is going to make it better is not making it better."

"I won't shut you out again. I put too much pressure on myself. Plus, the bullshit that was being reported."

"Tabitha."

"Tabitha was nothing but fake media. I was out eating at a restaurant and she approached me."

"I expect you made it clear with her that you're with someone correct?"

I grinned at her taking control and putting her foot down.

"I did, Mara. You don't have to worry about her ever doing something stupid again."

"Good. I would hate to have to move on and find someone else." She stood and removed her wet jacket and top, then slowly kicked off her shoes and unbuttoned her pants. She stood in front of me, wearing only her panties and bra.

"What are you doing?" I asked.

"Maybe if you follow me, you'll find out." She swished off toward my bedroom. I saw her remove her bra and drop it to the floor. A few seconds later, her panties followed. I licked my lips and followed her toward my bedroom, staring as she climbed on my bed and slowly crawled to the middle on her hands and knees.

$\mathcal{I}$ decided to make it known that this was going to be a one-and-done situation. No more being ignored and confused. He needed to decide and let me know where he stood with me because the brooding asshole attitude was done. Yes, he'd lost a huge game, but that didn't mean it was the end of the world.

I looked over my shoulder and saw him staring at me, so I decided to give him something to look forward to by sliding my index finger into my mouth, getting it wet, and moving it toward my pussy.

"Mara," he muttered, and I saw his eyes turn dark. Was I ready to feel him inside of me again? Could he be trusted with my heart fully? These were questions I debated about for the last few days and weeks.

"Yes."

"You look beautiful, baby."

"Come here."

"I want to watch you pleasure yourself."

My head fell back as I arched my back and stroked in and out, feeling my orgasm rise with every stroke. I gripped my breast with my free hand, squeezing and tweaking my nipples as I continued to masturbate in front of him.

He came toward me, caressing my ass, then down my legs and back up to my hips.

"So damn beautiful," Donovan said, hovering over my back. He was still wearing his shorts. His forehead fell to my shoulder, and he breathed heavily in my ear. "What are you doing to me?" he asked.

"I could ask you the same."

Donovan peppered kisses down my back and slapped me on the ass.

"Mmm…" A low groan left my mouth.

The scent of my arousal filled the room as my wetness started to seep into the sheets. Donovan pushed my hand away and replaced it with his own. Another finger traced up my belly button toward my breast. Slowly grinding on his erection, I reached behind me to stroke his girth through his shorts. "Take these off," I demanded.

"Lie flat on the bed."

Donovan rose off the bed, removed his shorts, and then came back to bed. He started kissing from my neck down to my ass. He spread my butt cheeks and danced over my pussy with his tongue.

I lifted my leg a little to give him more room. He inserted a finger and groaned. I reached out to grab the back of his neck, and my breath hitched.

"Donovan!" I whined, humping his face, as he drew my bud between his lips.

"You want to come, baby?"

"Yes, please."

"I promise to keep a smile on your face and never hurt your heart again." Donovan's lips grazed over me as I held his stare. He lined his dick up with my sex and pushed inside and gripped the bedsheets.

"Ahhh... I missed this, baby," Donovan rasped.

I heard our lovemaking around the room and his words came out in a growl as he picked up the pace.

"Fuuckkk...You've been the one all this time."

"I love you."

"I need you, Kamara. You're all I need, and I promise I'll never hurt you again." Donovan pulled out and turned me around to lie on my back. He hovered over my face and stared as his girth lined up with my sex, and he grinded back and forth. Our hips danced in a slow rhythm as my breath hitched, and I writhed underneath him. I almost felt like I was flying on a cloud when he pressed his mouth to mine, then trailed his tongue near my ear and whispered, "You're mine, Mara. No one will ever take your place." He entwined our hands together, breathing heavily.

"I'm coming!" I screamed, feeling the wetness between our joined lovemaking build up and seep onto the sheets. Donovan sped up and I heard his chants and pleading.

"Fuck! I'm about to come in you, sweetheart. Goddamn."

"I want to taste you." I sucked on his ear and he shook his head.

"I...I... Mara..." Donovan thrusted, gripped my neck gently and bit my bottom lip as I trembled from my release.

"Ugh.... Shit!" Donovan growled and spilled his seed and collapsed on top of me.

"Wow."

"Intense." Donovan moved off me and pulled me on top of his chest.

I ran a hand up and down his sweaty chest.

"I think you've made your point," I teased, lifting my

eyes to peer at him.

He grinned.

"Nothing else matters but you and me."

"We should shower and get some rest."

"I hate to move; you took all my energy," Donovan joked.

"Don't tell me big, bad Donovan Hunt has been undone by little old Mara Powell in bed," I teased, tapping his bottom lip with my index finger.

"That can't get out. I couldn't live it down if Reuben or Savion found out." He chuckled.

"Poor baby. Come on, let's grab a shower and find something to eat."

Feeling like our old selves again I rose up and kissed him again and moved out of his arms and headed to the bathroom. He groaned from behind and slapped me on the ass, then wrapped his hands around my waist.

"Welcome to my world. The first time we had sex, I thought my legs wouldn't work again."

He kissed the back of my neck and went to turn the water on in the shower and check the temperature.

"How is everything with the newspaper?"

"Great, my stories are making an impact."

"Did you figure out that issue with the Business district?" he asked.

Donovan stepped behind me in the shower and grabbed the lavender shower gel I used last time and a towel to wash my back.

"Yeah, the mayor was potentially going to have to step in if it went another way."

"Good, you're turning into our very own Barbara Walters."

I chortled at his comment.

"Far from Barbara Walters, but I do enjoy bringing to

light issues I see destroying our community."

"Were you really going to interview Julian?" Donovan questioned.

I had to think about that for a moment. A part of me could have done the interview for selfish reasons—either to get back at him or to gain more notice for my career. But I wasn't the type to get clout by chasing someone else's fame. Julian was using me to get back at Donovan, and I couldn't live with myself, knowing I had stooped to that level.

"No, it's not worth having him use me to get back at you. I'd rather not be with you if that's the case," I said.

He tensed up.

"I do apologize, you know that right," he said and turned me around in the shower and tilted my chin.

"I know and we're starting fresh. So, let me wash your back and then find something to cook for us."

"Good luck finding something; I haven't gone shopping for food in a week," Donovan said.

"What have you done for food?"

"Mostly eat out or dinner at my parents."

"Athletes." I grinned, pecked his lips, and grabbed the towel out of his hands, and he turned as I moved the towel across his shoulder and down his back. We stayed in the shower for another twenty minutes after having sex for a second time and eventually stepped out and changed into clothes.

"I see you have a little leftover pasta and beer." I shook my head in disbelief.

"We can order and have food delivered. Not in the mood to go out," Donovan said.

"Okay, what do you have a taste for?"

"You." He winked.

I pointed my finger at him.

"The kitchen is closed for the night, sir." I laughed.

He smirked, stood, and grabbed his phone off the table to put in an order for takeout.

*****

THE NEXT DAY I pulled into the empty parking space out in front of Cafe Sin and saw Terry rubbing the head of a dog. I got out of the car, grabbed my purse, and headed toward him.

"Nice to see you again Terry, where have you been hiding?"

"Pretty lady! I've been around. I stayed at the shelter since it was raining," he said.

"Who's your friend here?"

"This is Doggy," he said.

I bent down and rubbed Doggy's head.

"You couldn't think of any other name?"

"Just fit," Terry said and I laughed, watching the small black dog lick Terry's hand.

"Well, did you hear the good news? They're not tearing down this area," I said.

"That's wonderful, Kamara," Terry said.

"It's all because of you."

"No, you're the one who spoke up."

"Because you informed me, and I stood brave. So here you go as a thank you." I pulled out a hundred-dollar bill and tried to pass it to him and he blocked my hand.

"I can't take that, pretty lady."

"Why not? Is my money not good enough?"

"I was only trying to help. Wasn't looking for money."

"I understand, but you deserve this."

I stuffed the money in his pocket and went toward the coffee shop and opened the door to step inside. My phone vibrated, and I pulled it out of my pocket and saw that Donovan had texted me.

Donovan: Dinner tonight?

Me: Yes.

Donovan: Where are you?

Me: Grabbing coffee.

Donovan: You snuck out so fast, I couldn't enjoy breakfast.

Me: Your definition of "breakfast" would have been me on my back.

Donovan: The best meal of the day.

Me: Incorrigible.

Donovan: I'll pick you up for dinner.

Me: Okay, babe.

Donovan: Call me if you need anything.

Me: I will.

"Someone is happy today," Rodney said.

"Hi Rodney, can I get the usual please?"

"Sure, how have things been?" Rodney questioned.

"Things are great, where's Abigail?"

"In the back organizing inventory," Rodney replied.

"I just saw Terry and his new dog."

"Yeah, he tried to come in here with the dog and I had to tell him to stay outside and I'll bring him something to drink."

"He calls him Doggy."

"That's Terry for you." Rodney chortled, placed my cup on the counter and the barista started to make my latte as we continued talking.

"Did you see the papers today?" he asked.

"No, what happened?"

He walked away to the employee entrance of the shop and grabbed a newspaper that was sitting on the counter.

"Read the headlines." Rodney slapped the paper in my hand. I opened it up and gasped at the headlines.

"*City Council Being Indicted for Fraud,*" I muttered.

"Yeah, I had the same reaction," Rodney said.

"I guess the constant attention we brought had the authorities wanting to check out what was happening."

"I agree. So, hopefully, we can get back to normal."

"I thought I heard your voice." Abigail came around from the back and hugged me.

"Rodney said you were doing inventory."

"Usually on a Friday we end up having double the inventory at both shops. Running back and forth," Abigail explained and I nodded.

The barista placed my drink on the counter, and I picked it up and took a sip.

"Heading to the office?" Abigail questioned.

"I am longing to write and looking for the next piece of news to report."

"Did everything work out with you and D?"

I smiled and nodded.

"I like that smile on you, friend. Keep it up."

"Me too, but we'll talk soon. I have to get going," I replied and hugged her again. I waved at Rodney as I got in my car and drove off.

I made it to the office before nine with light traffic. I sat at my desk and turned on my computer, placing my purse on the floor and looking over my emails. An email came through with the subject, *"Guest interview for Julian Anderson",* and I deleted it before even reading it because I knew he was just trying to start drama that I didn't need. I sat back in my seat and pulled out my notepad, then started making lists of things I could potentially start talking about in my next column. I sipped on my coffee as I worked for the rest of the day on my next passion project.

DONOVAN

"Donovan, over here! Donovan, are you ready to get back into the game?" a reporter asked.

I shut the door to my jeep, locked it, and pulled my gym bag over my shoulder. I ignored the questions as I walked into the stadium for practice. The coach had called a meeting before practice and hopefully it wouldn't be long so I could make it to dinner with Kamara that night. I wanted to take her out on the town like a normal couple and not get harassed, but I doubted that was possible. Already on social media I'd seen posts of her going into my condo building the other night, and people were making claims that we had eloped. I couldn't make that stuff up, and the constant badgering was giving me a headache.

"No comment."

"Are you planning on proposing to your girlfriend?"

"No comment."

"What about your interview with Ben Simmons?"

"Ben got what he wanted—some face-time with me. I can't fault him for wanting to speak with the best of the

177

best." I smirked, walking through the front door and leaving them screaming more questions at my back.

I saw one of the security guards and slapped hands with him.

"I got my money on you for the next big game, man," Jonee, the security guard, said.

"Thanks Jonee, I got you this time."

I pushed open the employee entrance door and headed to the locker room. I dropped my bag on the floor and opened my locker.

A few guys stood around, talking and joking back and forth, as music played.

"D! You know Coach is on a rampage man, be careful," Steven, the defensive player, said.

"Already on the Coach's shit list. This is just another mark," I joked, shrugged my shoulders, lifted my shirt, and put on a plain shirt and shorts for practice.

"I thought you'd be late," I said to Savion.

He strolled over and removed his headphones.

"Sutton asked me to keep talking and shit," he fussed.

"You're at the 'talking' stage as a couple?" I bent over and laughed.

He flicked me on the side of my head. "Fuck you, man," Savion said, putting his bag on the ground and changing his shorts and shoes.

"What's this meeting about?" Reuben walked inside drinking a cup of water.

"Probably about you needing to get tested," Steven joked and the room erupted in laughs.

"Oh, well tell your mom to call me for the Doctor's number," Reuben responded, Steven lunged at him, and we blocked him from fighting.

"You know Reuben's messing with you man," Savion said, clapping Steven on the shoulder to calm him down.

"Am I?" Reuben said.

"Reuben, shut up and get ready for practice," Coach said, surprising us all.

"Yes, sir, Coach," Reuben replied.

"I called you all in to talk about a strategy for the next time we make it to the Super Bowl. We can't fumble like that again." Coach stared at me as he spoke.

"Donovan wasn't good, you know the reason," Walter brought up.

I stood ready to smack Walter across the face for bringing up old shit.

"Walter, you act like you've had a perfect game. I could have sworn they call you 'Butterfingers' since you can't hold shit for long," I said.

"That's enough, we're a team and no more back and forth instigating. I want everyone on their game from now on," Coach explained.

"Yes, sir!" we all said.

"Practice will be twice a week, more studying the plays and tapes. In order for us to get back to our status we need to show why we're the best to beat," Coach explained.

"Gotcha Coach," Savion replied.

"Donovan, run the plays with Savion and Reuben. Eat, breathe, live football," Coach said and handed me the playbook.

I nodded, grabbed the football, and headed out to the field to throw the ball around.

* * *

I PICKED Kamara up after practice and went straight to my place to shower and change, while she changed in the other room. I asked her to bring a bag with her to spend the weekend with me, so we could spend some time together while she had a break between writing. I still had practice to deal with on and off.

Kamara was dressed in a light beige, flowing dress with a black shawl around her arms, showing off her thick figure. I held the door to Che's Indian Restaurant open and let her walk in first, then stopped at the hostess desk.

"Welcome to Che's, do you have a reservation?" she asked.

The place was new in town and I wanted to try something different with less notice from the photographers. Sutton recommended this place a while back and I was now getting around to trying the food.

"I called earlier for Donovan Hunt."

She checked the books and pointed at my name.

"Mr. Hunt we have your table ready for you." She escorted us to the table with the window to our backs. I held the chair out for Kamara to take a seat and ran a hand across her soft skin and inhaled the sweet aroma of cinnamon from her perfume.

"Your waitress will be out shortly," she said, laying the menus down for us.

"Thanks."

"This is a nice place, Donovan," Mara said.

"I'm glad you like it, baby."

"You didn't seem like the Indian food type of person."

She cupped her hand under her cheek.

"I'm trying new things because of you."

"Good, I like that. Maybe I can get you to sit long enough to watch my favorite movie."

"Babe there's only so many times I can watch *Coming to America*." I chuckled.

"You can never go wrong with an Eddie Murphy movie."

"That's true, but I'd rather make my own movie with you." I winked at her and scanned the menu.

"Not going to happen, buddy. Let me order for you."

"Sure, just make sure to order a lot. Starving after practice."

"How was that?"

"Long and annoying."

"Please tell me you didn't fight with anyone."

"No."

"That look in your eyes says differently."

"Hello, I'm Capri and I'll be your waitress today."

"Hi, can we get chicken masala, malai kofi, and pala paneer? Plus, naan, and two glasses of water and a bottle of Riesling," Mara ordered.

I sat back, watching her take charge, and it made my dick hard.

Capri continued writing everything down, and then lifted our menus and walked off to grab our water and wine.

"Work was good for you today?" I questioned, covering her hand with mine on top of the table.

"It was busy mostly. Cailey was out of the office mostly."

"What about Luna? She hasn't hit me up in a while."

"Luna's being Luna. You know your sister is either shopping or with some guy," Mara joked.

"Reuben showed up at practice, so it wasn't him this time."

"How do you feel about them dating?"

"I can't say anything. I'm dating you."

I hadn't even thought of Luna's opinion on me and Mara dating because we're both adults and Luna's never told me to stay away from her friends before.

"Have you spoken to your parents lately?"

"No, I'll go see them soon. Tonight is about us reconnecting and focusing on our future."

"I like the sound of that," she said.

I leaned over the table and pressed a kiss on her lips.

"Don't you start something in this restaurant. You'll end up having us on the homepage of the celebrity blogs." She giggled.

"This time it's worth it." I pressed another kiss and licked her bottom lick. Capri walked back over.

"Two waters and a bottle of wine. Your meal will be out shortly, starting with naan and samosa," Capri said and placed each dish on the table as I grabbed my napkin to place on my lap and we dug in and fed each other.

The night was a success, and I came back to my condo watching Kamara on her knees taking my dick down the back of her throat. I gripped the back of her head as she played with her pussy and moaned. I closed my eyes and prayed we'd be like this forever until my last breath.

"All mine," I mumbled to myself.

Today had been another day of practice and dealing with the media, questioning whether we'd make it to the next step and win the championship game that was coming up. I didn't like talking to them; all they wanted was a sound bite that they could play on repeat to bash you.

I decided to get up and drive over to Kamara's place to see what she was doing. The last time we spoke, she had just gotten back from shopping with my sister and planned on having lunch with her parents. I pulled over to the side of her building and parked, leaving the car running.

"What the fuck am I doing?" My phone rang as my head dipped over the steering wheel.

I picked it up and answered. "Yeah."

"You're an idiot."

I pulled the phone away from my face and looked at the caller ID. Savion was the one person I could always count on to tell me the truth. No matter what I did good or bad he'd keep it real with me.

"What are you talking about?" I questioned if I was doing the right thing by just showing up without calling.

"Not only did we lose the game, but you lost your mind." I fixed my eyes on her apartment building and wondered if she saw the last game we lost. I called her right after, we talked for a few hours, and she helped me to see I was trying to carry a load of responsibility on my shoulders to live up to an impossible ideal of being the best.

"I know."

"Then get your shit together and go see her."

"I'm outside her place right now."

"So why the hell are you still on the phone with me?"

"I'm a fool and annoyed at myself again."

"You fucked up Donovan I won't lie, but she's forgiven you, bro."

"Thanks. I guess."

"Take my advice and go see your woman, have dinner, and release some stress," he said.

I hung up, stepped out of the car, and went to knock on her door.

"Hey, baby." She stood on her toes and kissed me, wrapping her arms around my neck.

I shut the door with my leg and cupped her ass.

I heard someone clear their throat.

"Big fan, Mr. Hunt," said a guy who looked homeless, holding a dog.

"Uhm, hello." I peered at Kamara with my eyes wide.

"Donovan this is Terry, a friend."

"A friend."

"He lives around the corner from Cafe Sin and I usually help him out with food or clothes. He's homeless."

"Oh."

"I was just leaving," Terry said.

"Are you sure? I can order food for you, and we can have lunch," I said.

"We already ate, babe. I saw him after I came back from shopping."

"My belly's full, thanks again pretty lady," Terry stated and I opened the door for him again.

He left. I looked back at Mara again in surprise.

"What?" she questioned.

"Mara you're too nice."

"What do you mean?"

"Bringing a homeless guy into your home? I'm not sure that's a good idea."

"Terry's harmless, what are you doing here anyway?" She pulled me over to the couch and I sat next to her, then pulled her onto my lap needing to feel her warmth around me.

"I was missing you, but I see you already moved on to another man."

"Stop fussing. Terry's a nice guy and he's helped me out a lot."

"Fine. You smell good, though." I nuzzled my face against her neck.

She giggled.

"You didn't come all the way over here for sex, did you?" She pulled back and looked at me with a raised brow.

"No, I just needed to be in your presence."

"Well, I have work to do babe, so you're going to have to entertain yourself." Mara stood and grabbed her drink off the table and went to the kitchen.

"Move in with me," I blurted out and she gasped in shock.

"Huh?"

"Move in with me."

"You serious?"

I followed and cupped both her cheeks.

"I've never been more serious in my life."

"That means we would wake up together and go to sleep together every night."

"I know."

"It means you'll see all of my weird quirks with my green facial mask, rollers in my hair, nightguard," she explained, and I laughed.

"Baby I want all of that and more."

"You want to really live together? I mean as a committed couple, pay bills together?"

"You don't have to pay bills."

"I'm not letting you pay for me, Donovan."

"Fine, you can pay a bill, but I just need you near me. The nights of us splitting our time back and forth at our places is draining and I hate when you get up and leave me."

"Okay."

"Really?" I leaned down to stare into her eyes for confirmation.

"Yes, let's move in together." She smiled and poked her lips out for a kiss.

I lifted her and spun her around the kitchen as she laughed.

"You're the best thing that has ever happened to me, Kamara."

"I feel the same way, Donovan."

One month later, I set down the last box of Kamara's items that she had brought to our official place together. That was weird for me to say in my head, but it was a beautiful thing. I loved repeating it to myself, and anyone else who would listen. We were living together officially, as a couple that was in love, and even though our jobs would sometimes clash, I wouldn't let it take away from how much she meant to me, and vice versa. The living room was already looking different, with some of her furniture woven in, like her favorite pictures. I had her office set up in the spare guest room. Since I rarely had people over, we redid it for her to have a place to work in peace.

Luna was there, along with Sutton and Savion. Reuben had a family thing and couldn't make it, but we planned on having a housewarming party with everyone and our parents one day the upcoming week.

After I asked her to move in with me, we'd planned on moving her in quickly, but our time was limited. I had away games back-to-back, and she ended up getting a bigger position at the newspaper as the Senior Editor after Cailey took over a position at a bigger paper and left. Now, Kamara was running things, and I was more than proud of her for taking the big leap.

"Where does this go?" Luna asked, holding a colorful vase with pictures of animals across it.

"In my office please," Mara said.

"Are you guys seeing this?" Savion said, and turned the TV up louder. I turned and looked at what he was talking about and my mouth dropped open in surprise. Julian Anderson was being escorted out of his home in handcuffs and they say he was dealing drugs.

"OMG!" Luna gasped.

I saw a reporter post a photo of Mara, along with her name. I scrolled down to the byline at the bottom and saw it was written by the same writer who had exposed the drug deal.

"Mara you did this?" Luna said as Mara nonchalantly looked up and shrugged.

"My job."

"Baby, you just put the biggest football star in jail."

"I look at it as a story, no one is above the story." She winked.

"Come here." I lifted her hands and pressed a kiss on the back of her palm and watched as Ben Simmons came on next.

"We have to really take a moment and look at this. Would this null and void the win?" Ben asked.

"I would say the league would need to investigate," Charles responded.

I continued watching until a knock on my door came and I figured that was the food I ordered. I dropped her hands and opened the door to see my food in the hands of the last person I needed to show up.

"Mr. Hunt, I wanted to personally deliver your food, sir."

"Thanks, but you could have let them bring it up to me."

"I-"

She started to speak, but Mara cut her off and yanked the bag out her hand.

"Your personal delivery services are no longer needed. I suggest you find someone to try and sleep with because this one belongs to me," Mara told her and slammed the door in her face. I grinned and she rolled her eyes at me.

"I belong to you?"

"Do I belong to you?" she countered.

"You're everything I want and need, Kamara Powell." I took the food out of her hands and placed it on the couch and picked her up in my arms and she wrapped her legs around my waist, and we tongued each other down.

"Can't you two wait until your company leaves?" Sutton asked.

"Take the food and go," Mara replied and I laughed, hearing her taking charge. My baby put her foot down and this was a new Mara that I hadn't seen before.

* * *

LATER IN THE EVENING, we were eating dinner. Her legs were strewn across my lap, and she was dressed in one of my t-shirts. I was in my boxers. Luna, Sutton, and Savion had left once we went to the bedroom. They left the food in the fridge, and we heated it up. It was pasta, baked fish, steamed vegetables, and chicken. She had me watching *Mean Girls* for the 10th time, and I was ready to block it from my cable channel. I massaged her feet and kissed the back of her ankle, as she closed her eyes and her head fell back against the couch.

"Mmm. This is so good."

"Any pasta left?" I questioned.

She nodded and put a small amount on the fork, then pushed it toward me. "Good, right?"

"It is; we have to order from them again."

"We have so much to put away." She sighed as she looked around the living room.

"We'll get it done."

"How are you feeling about the upcoming season?" she asked.

"I feel good, the amount of practice we get in as a team is helping."

"Good, I'm excited to get back to watching you from the box suite. Here try this." She pushed more pasta my way.

"Thanks baby."

"I love you."

"I love you more, now can we watch something else. I've had enough of Regina George."

She giggled and I shook my head and continued massaging her feet and ran a hand up her thigh and took the plate out of her hand, placing it on the table.

"Donovan Hunt are you trying to seduce me?" she asked.

"Is it working?"

"Depends."

"On what?"

"If you can stay awake long enough to watch *Love Jones*." She laughed, and I shook my head, tickled her as she squirmed in my arms and bent down and kissed her lips as she moaned.

"Mara."

"Yes…"

"Never change," I said, and she wrapped her arms around my neck.

"You're all I need, Donovan Hunt."

K amara
Two Years Later

I tried to squeeze into my favorite pair of pants, and I had no luck because of the weight gain. I looked in the mirror, and then down at the reason I was no longer my usual self. I spotted the round belly that poked out, taunting me about one of the days I'd forgotten to take my birth control pill. I was now pregnant with Donovan Hunt's baby, and on the national stage as his girlfriend in the middle of another playoff game. It was kismet that we made it back to the same place that really launched my career and put him on the map as the superstar quarterback of a football team. Even when I tried to resist his charms and push him away, he broke through and made me believe that not all athletes were arrogant to the point where they didn't see what was right in front of their eyes.

Today, I was heading to the stadium with Luna to watch his game in the private booth with our family and friends. Then we'd come back home and have dinner. After moving in together, I had gotten used to the housekeepers and butlers—even though I wanted to cook meals for him and start our own traditions. But he said once the baby came, then we'd make our own traditions.

"You ready?" Luna poked her head into our bedroom.

I nodded, picking up my ID badge and purse. I slid my arms into my jacket and followed her downstairs and out of the fifteen thousand square-foot mini mansion to the car that was reserved for the family. I'd told Donovan he didn't need to do this, but once again he insisted since I was traveling with precious cargo.

"I'm hungry; I hope they have my favorite foods." I rubbed my stomach, thinking of the hot dogs and barbequed ribs that the chef had put out the last time I went to a game.

Lately, every muscle in my body wanted to lay out and sleep instead of work, but I knew as the senior editor, I had a responsibility to get my stories told quickly and precisely. Today was no exception—even though my boyfriend was leading the team to the national championship.

"Donovan probably has the entire room setup with all the food you love to eat." Luna typed away on her phone.

"Leave my baby out of this and you aren't innocent either in this."

She lifted her head and met my eyes as the car pulled out of the driveway toward the stadium in downtown Los Angeles.

"Says the woman that's six months pregnant," Luna teased, reaching over to rub my belly.

I smacked her hand away and flipped her off, regretting wearing jeans and a long sweater. The weather was pretty nice out, and I'd hate to sweat through my clothes on national TV—especially if the team won, and I got a chance to interview them for my column. "Don't be jealous; your time will come soon."

The black SUV made it to the stadium a few minutes later, and the driver parked and got out to open our door. I stepped out first, then Luna, to the awaiting flashbulbs of the cameras. Even if I was a part of the media, I didn't like the way they hounded people to get a story, and I'd made a promise to myself to treat everyone the same—even celebrities and athletes.

Luna locked arms with me, and we jetted inside the stadium. We stepped toward the elevator and waited for it to head up to the private suite that Donovan had reserved.

"Can you believe this is his third championship game?" Luna commented when my phone rang and I wanted to ignore it, but I knew my family was meeting us here and I wanted to make sure they found the correct suite room. I picked it up, smiled hearing my mom's soft voice.

"Baby we made it here," Mother said.

"Oh, that was quick. I just stepped on the elevator with Luna going to the suite now."

"That's fine, just have Donovan send someone to get us."

"Are you sure?" I lied, not really wanting to turn around and go back down on the elevator to escort them back up here. We made it to the front door with security standing outside. Luna waved her badge, and they opened the door for her, and she nudged me to go first. I strolled in with my head down, finger in my ear trying to block out the noise in the background.

"Surprise!" I jumped back, mouth wide open in shock, looked over my shoulder at Luna, then toward my Mom standing in front of me. I closed my mouth, glanced at my phone again and they laughed.

"Wh... What...How?" I stuttered, not understanding

what was happening right now. I raised my hand to my forehead.

"Donovan wanted to have everyone here for the surprise," she said, and he walked into the room and again I was shocked because I thought he was suited and ready to head out to the field.

"Donovan...What are you doing here?"

My entire body heated up. I didn't know what was going on. Everybody around me held up their phones and cameras to take pictures. Then Donovan dropped to his knee, and my eyes widened in surprise. He reached over and grasped my hand, pressing a kiss to my knuckles. My stomach dropped, my eyes watered, and I clasped my free hand over my mouth.

"Baby, we've come a long way and I wouldn't be the man I am today without your strength."

"Are you for real?" I whimpered, wiping the tears that trickled down my cheek.

Everyone chuckled at my expense.

"I love you and I want to spend the rest of my life showing you how much you mean to me. Will you marry me Kamara and make me the happiest man in the world?" he asked, and I was speechless for a second and then nodded.

"Answer the man!" I heard from the crowd, and they laughed.

"Yes! I'll marry you, Donovan, and I love you, too," I responded.

He stood and cupped my face, then kissed my lips. He pulled back to slide the ring on my finger.

"When did you do this?" I questioned and reached up to clasp the back of his neck, standing on my tiptoes.

"A man never tells his secrets baby or shall I say Mrs. Hunt," Donovan teased, pecking me on the mouth.

The both of us grinned and I looked at the ring, then my fiancé and kissed him again on the mouth.

"Thank you Mr. Hunt and I can't wait for the twins to get here," I replied, surprising him along with our families. I'd gone to the doctor with Luna and they told me I was carrying twins and I debated on when to tell him. Now was the perfect time and the best motivation to win the champion game.

"Twins?" Donovan's eyes fluttered in shock.

"Yep. Get ready for two little ones running around."

"She—She—She's having twins," Donovan said.

The crowd clapped, hugging us joyfully. I let everyone rub my belly and take pictures as we talked about the ring and the wedding. I wouldn't add any more stress to my plate with a wedding until after the babies got here. But it was more than enough for me to continue my goals as a journalist, a wife, and a mom.

"I love you, Kamara. More than you know," Donovan said.

"I love you, too, Donovan Hunt. Now, go win the game, baby. You're not the only one planning on being MVP today," I teased. I blew him a kiss as he started to leave the box to head downstairs and play. I relaxed with our families, enjoying the conversations that flowed in the room and eating to my heart's content.

* * *

I HOPE you enjoyed Kamara and Donovan's story. If you want more "Contemporary Romance, why not try *Heart of Stone Series" Click here* https://books2read.com/u/boWPAV

Have you read *"Temptation" yet ? Click here* https://

books2read.com/u/mle1Vv That is a standalone contemporary, sports, curvy girl romance.

Please also check out my Dark Mafia Series *"Antonio and Sabrina Struck In Love"* https://books2read.com/u/bzjYAE with a host of characters intertwined.

ORDER OF SERIES

Heart of Stone Book 1 Emery and Jackson
https://books2read.com/u/boWPAV

Heart of Stone Book 1.5
https://books2read.com/u/mKELYZ

Heart of Stone Book 2 Jordan and Damon
https://books2read.com/u/ba2OMx

Heart of Stone Book 3.5 Bottoms Up
https://books2read.com/u/4EkjBg

Heart of Stone Book 3 Angela and Brent
https://books2read.com/u/31rx9l

Heart of Stone Book 4 Jessica and Joseph
https://books2read.com/u/4NXyPG

The Early Years: A Prequel to Antonio & Sabrina: Struck in Love

https://books2read.com/u/49Zjnw

Antonio & Sabrina: Struck in Love, Books 1

https://books2read.com/u/4AxKLo

Antonio & Sabrina: Struck in Love, Books 2

https://books2read.com/u/bpED6g

Antonio & Sabrina: Struck in Love, Books 3

https://books2read.com/u/3LpgdJ

Janice & Carlo: Captivated By His Love

https://books2read.com/u/b6je6M

Antonio & Sabrina: Struck in Love, Book 4

https://books2read.com/u/4NQyE9

Joaquin Fuertes (The Fuertes Cartel, Books 1)

https://books2read.com/u/mvZlgV

Joaquin Fuertes (The Fuertes Cartel, Books 2)

https://books2read.com/u/4DWwLd

Antonio & Sabrina: Struck in Love, Book 5

https://books2read.com/u/b5kZ8O

The Carrington Cartel

By Chiquita Dennie:
Temptation
Antonio & Sabrina: Struck in Love, Books 1, 2, 3
Janice & Carlo: Captivated by His Love
Heart of Stone, Book 1: Emery & Jackson
Heart of Stone, Book 1.5: Emery & Jackson, A Valentine's Day Short Story
Heart of Stone, Book 2: Jordan & Damon
Heart of Stone, Book 3: Angela & Brent

By Keke Renée:
Wet Heat
His Peace, Her Pleasure
Baby, It's Cold Outside
Love Don't Live Here Anymore, Book 1
Every Time We Touch (A Wet Heat Novelette)
By Ava S. King
Agent Red-Fatal Memory(Teagan Stone Book 1)
Agent Red-Fatal Target(Teagan Stone Book 2)

ABOUT THE AUTHOR

Chiquita Dennie is an Author, Filmmaker, Podcast host, and Entrepreneur. Born in Memphis, TN, and a Los Angeles CA native. Her background in film/tv has taught and shaped her passion for screenwriting with her suspense script Antonio and Sabrina, that turned into romance novel Antonio and Sabrina Struck In Love Series. Since its debut, fans have embraced the unconventional love story and Chiquita has gone on to create more unfor-gettable couples with Heart of Stone series. Making both series Amazon BestSellers. She writes contemporary steamy romance, romantic suspense, women's fiction, fantasy and so much more.

Want to know what happens next?

Follow me on my website to catch the next release.

Reviews are the lifeblood of the publishing world. They're read, appreciated, and needed.

Please consider taking the time to leave a few words on your review platform of choice.

Sign up for updates and sneak peaks at the site below. www.chiquitadennie.com

PLAYLIST

1.Beyonce: 7/11
   2.Rihanna: Cockiness
   3.Heather Headley: In My Mind
   4.Imagine Dragons: Radioactive
   5.Tank: When We
   6.Jazmine Sullivan: Insecure
   7.Rick James & Teena Marie: Fire and Desire
   8.The Temptations: Ain't Too Proud To Beg
   9.The Supremes: You Keep Hanging On
   10.Rihanna: Love On The Brain

The home of authors African American, Interracial, Women's Fiction, Fantasy, Erotic, and Contemporary Romance novels. Along with Thriller, Suspense, Poetry, Beauty, and Style Books. Thank you for taking the time out to visit. Join our mailing list to stay updated with new releases and blog posts.

ACKNOWLEDGMENTS

I want to dedicate this to my team that helps me behind the scenes, from my editors, test readers, graphic designers, and the list goes on. Truly appreciate each of you for keeping me on my toes.

www.ingramcontent.com/pod-product-compliance
Lightning Source LLC
Chambersburg PA
CBHW070938190726
48292CB00004B/1232